Praise fo

"For intelligent intrigu_____ved
by moments of humor,_____ and *The Traitor's Daughter*."—Romance R___ws Today

"*The Traitor's Daughter* is a beguiling combination of romance and suspense, leavened with deft humor. Debut author Elizabeth Powell gives readers a spirited, original heroine, an honorable gentleman who is a true hero, and enough sparks to light a bonfire. I highly recommend *The Traitor's Daughter*. This book may well be a contender for best Regency romance of the year."—America Online's Romance Fiction Forum

1.

A Reckless Bargain

2. The Reluctant Rogue

Elizabeth Powell

A SIGNET BOOK

SIGNET
Published by New American Library, a division of
Penguin Putnam Inc., 375 Hudson Street,
New York, New York 10014, U.S.A
Penguin Books Ltd, 80 Strand,
London WC2R 0RL, England
Penguin Books Australia Ltd, Ringwood
Victoria, Australia
Penguin Books Canada Ltd, 10 Alcorn Avenue,
Toronto, Ontario, Canada M4V 3B2
Penguin Books (N.Z.) Ltd, 182–190 Wairau Road,
Auckland 10, New Zealand

Penguin Books Ltd, Registered Offices:
Harmondsworth, Middlesex, England

First published by Signet, an imprint of New American Library,
a division of Penguin Putnam Inc.

First Printing, August 2002
10 9 8 7 6 5 4 3 2 1

PUBLISHER'S NOTE
This is a work of fiction. Names, characters, places, and incidents either are the
product of the author's imagination or are used fictitiously, and any resemblance to
actual persons, living or dead, business establishments, events, or locales is entirely
coincidental.

To my husband, Bill,
who will always be my hero.

Chapter One

Bath
June, 1813

*P*liny, Plutarch, Quintilian . . . She frowned. Where was Pope? He had been here just a moment ago; she would swear to it. She checked again. Pope had gone missing.

Her lower lip caught between her teeth, her brow furrowed with concentration, Kit Mallory stood atop the rickety stepladder, sorting through an awkward armful of leather-bound books, when she heard the library door creak open.

"Mrs. Mallory, I would speak with you!" exclaimed an imperious voice.

Oh, no. Not again.

Kit started, her grip loosened, and the books tumbled from her arms to land with several tumultuous thumps on the floor below. The ladder swayed, and she made a mad grab for the railings. She righted herself, then stood stock-still for several moments, her pulse pounding loudly in her ears, her eyes closed against a sudden wave of dizziness as the room, ladder and all, seemed to tilt beneath her.

Gooseflesh prickled over her skin as she realized just how close she'd come to falling. And with the realization came a rush of anger. She looked down at the books heaped at the base of the ladder and exhaled slowly; none of them appeared to be damaged. She twisted around to glare at the intruder. "I told you before, the answer is—oh!"

A familiar figure stood in the doorway, but not the one she was expecting. Tall and angular, in a round gown of vibrant purple silk trimmed with teal velvet ribbons, with dozens of strands of pearls looped around her long, wrinkled neck, the lady commanded one's immediate attention. Soft curls of gray hair protruded from beneath her turban, a creation of teal silk adorned with a diamond brooch and three immense plumes. Sharp black eyes and a rather prominent nose gave her a striking, but not unhandsome countenance.

"Your Grace!" Kit gasped, horrified by her rudeness. "Forgive me. I had no idea you were here."

"So I gathered," replied the Dowager Duchess of Wexcombe, unruffled. "The fault is mine, child, for startling you so. Now come down from there at once, before you do yourself an injury."

Kit descended the ladder with gingerly steps. "You might have given me a little warning, ma'am. These volumes are irreplaceable." She knelt to collect the fallen tomes, then started to pile them on a nearby chair.

"Stop fussing with those books, girl, and pay attention." The elderly woman raised her gold-rimmed lorgnette and eyed Kit up and down. "Goodness, what on earth have you been doing? You look like a sparrow that has been bathing in the dust all day."

Kit brushed her hands against her drab brown skirt and pushed a few stray locks of hair from her eyes. "Not quite all day, Your Grace."

"Hmph," sniffed the duchess, her lips compressed in a thin line as she turned her attention to the floor-to-ceiling bookshelves that lined the room, then to the haphazard stacks that teetered atop almost every table and chair. She held out a lacy, embroidered kerchief. "There is a smudge on your nose."

Obediently, Kit took the cambric square and daubed at the offending mark.

"Really, Mrs. Mallory," Her Grace continued, "you cannot keep yourself locked up day after day with these moldy old books. 'Tis most unnatural."

"I do believe Your Grace has made your disapproval known on more than one occasion."

The older lady arched an eyebrow. "Are you being impertinent?"

Try as she might, Kit could not keep the corners of her mouth from twitching. "Oh, yes, ma'am. Every day, and as often as possible."

The duchess laughed and held out her gloved hands. "Saucebox. How glad I am to see you again. Do you never tire of this little game of mine?"

"Never." Kit took the lady's hands in her own and gave them a fond squeeze. "I was beginning to despair, thinking you were not coming. I trust you are well?"

"Well enough, considering my age and my temper."

Kit grinned. "And how was your trip from London?"

"Cold, wet, and thoroughly unpleasant," replied the duchess with asperity. "I vow it must have rained the entire time—mud up to one's ankles! But I did not come here to bore you with such stories; we have important matters to discuss. Will you invite me to take tea with you, or must I ring for the servants myself?"

"Best to let me do it; you will terrify them," Kit replied with a chuckle, then led her guest to the drawing room.

While Kit rang for tea, the dowager duchess seated herself on the lion-footed sofa by the hearth. The lady smoothed her skirts, then examined the room through her lorgnette. "You have made a few improvements to the place."

Kit lowered herself onto the rosewood chair opposite the duchess. "The house seemed so . . . so bare and colorless, and I couldn't stand it any longer. My late husband's solicitor thinks it barbaric—oh, he is too polite to say as much, but I can see it in the way his face puckers up like a prune whenever he steps through the front door. But I have never given a fig for the fickle dictates of fashion. This is my home, and I shall do as I please."

The duchess nodded, and the plumes on her turban nodded with her. "As it should be. You are no milk-and-water miss, and this house was in desperate need of some character."

Character? Kit allowed herself a small chuckle. Most gently reared ladies would gasp and turn pale—if not faint outright—at the pagan splendors of her drawing room, which included a carved sandalwood screen, a tiger-skin rug, and colorful Hindu masks on the walls. Sensuous stone goddesses graced the wall on either side of the hearth. Woven rugs in brilliant hues covered the floor. Fragrant wisps of flowery incense curled from a brass burner on the mantelpiece. The rest of the Georgian-style residence was decorated in much the same way, or it would be once she finished unpacking.

"If I could have, I would have brought along the whole

of Calcutta," she replied. Her smile began to fade around the edges.

"Do you miss India very much?" Through the lorgnette, the duchess's eyes appeared unnaturally large.

"It was the only place I ever felt truly at home."

Those large eyes softened. "A pity your situation would not allow you to remain."

Kit laced her fingers in her lap to stop their nervous fidgets. Her Grace was coming painfully close to subjects she would rather not discuss. "Since I could not stay, I decided to bring with me what I could. Do you like it?"

"It suits you." The duchess gave her a long, measured look, then gestured to the tall, multiarmed bronze statue visible in the vestibule. "Tell me—who is that rather large fellow out in the hall?"

Kit relaxed her clenched hands. "Come now, Your Grace. Did you never visit any temples in India? That is Lord Siva, the god of destruction and new beginnings. He is the patron deity of those who have no place in society—outcasts, and the like. Given all that has transpired over the course of my life, I thought it appropriate to set him in a place of honor."

The dowager frowned and opened her mouth to reply, but at that moment Ramesh, the imposing Hindu butler, brought in a tea tray laden with a steaming pot and clinking china cups, accompanied by an assortment of sweets. The turbaned, mahogany-skinned servant set the tray on the low table between the two ladies, pressed his large palms together in a reverent salute, then departed, all in silence.

The duchess stared after him through her lorgnette. "Gracious . . . I had forgotten you brought your servants with you."

"There is only Ramesh and his wife Lakshmi," Kit

replied. "They insisted on coming with me. Though, after the cold spring we had, I wonder if they have regretted that decision."

"Indeed?" murmured the duchess in a thoughtful tone, tapping the tip of one finger against her pointed chin. Then she shook herself and tucked her lorgnette into her oversize reticule. "And now we must get to the business at hand."

Kit's hand hesitated on the handle of the teapot. "What business would that be, Your Grace?"

"Why, your future, my dear."

"My future?" Kit echoed. Still somewhat shaky from the incident on the ladder, she managed to pour a cup of the fragrant tea without splashing any onto the saucer, then handed it to her guest.

The elderly woman heaved a sigh. "Yes, your future. I shall speak plainly, child, since I know no other way to go about it. You cannot continue to live like this."

"Like what?"

The dowager paused to sip her tea. "Like . . . well, like a hermit."

"A hermit?" Kit's frown deepened. She was turning into a veritable parrot; one would think her incapable of uttering a single word of her own.

"A hermit," confirmed the duchess with a nod. "A recluse. Like those fellows you told me about on our voyage . . . the ones who wander off into the wilderness and deny themselves any form of pleasure at all. Oh, what do you call them—"

"Ascetics. And I am not one of them, I assure you."

"What would you call it, then?" demanded the older woman. "You have not gone out into society at all, not to the assemblies or the concerts, or even to take the waters at the Pump Room. You keep your nose so buried in those foreign texts of yours that it's a wonder you haven't wasted completely away."

Good heavens . . . How did the duchess know all of this? Kit looked askance at her guest. "If I did not know better, Your Grace," she said archly, "I'd swear you have been checking up on me."

"And what if I have? I am not naturally disposed to interfering in people's lives, my dear, but enough is enough. I will not let you waste any more of your youth shut up like a nun in a cloister."

Kit sat in stunned silence, her cup halfway to her slack mouth.

"When I first met you aboard the *Daphne*," Her Grace continued, "I thought you an impertinent hussy. But you were the only one who ventured to speak to me; the rest of that craven lot could not even conceive that an august personage such as myself might be lonely and desire some company. If not for you, my dear, I do not think I would have survived the voyage from Calcutta." Moisture gleamed at the corners of the dowager's dark eyes.

Kit shuddered at the thought of that horrific passage, of the storms that battered the *Daphne* as it passed through the Cape of Good Hope, of the dark, pitching sea, the howling wind, and the terrible creaking of the ship's timbers. She had nursed the elderly duchess through debilitating bouts of *mal de mer* when the lady's own servants had been too ill to tend her, and the ordeal had forged an enduring bond of friendship between them. As a result, Kit held the duchess as dear as her own grandmother, despite the lady's tendency to speak her mind and meddle in the affairs of others.

"You give me too much credit, Your Grace," she protested. "I did no less than anyone else would have done."

The dowager sat straight up and glared down her aquiline nose. "Nonsense. You are an exceptional creature, and I will not permit you to wither away into a disappointed old maid." Her lips twitched. "You cannot expect happiness to come to you; you must seize it."

When she was in this sort of mood, any attempt to resist the imperious old lady was like trying to row against the current. "What do you suggest?" Kit asked cautiously.

The older woman appeared to consider the question. "Well, first of all, we must have you fitted for a new wardrobe. You're a fetching thing, but your looks will be greatly improved once you cast off those dreary gowns you insist on wearing."

Kit fingered the dull brown material of her sleeve. "Given that I am still unpacking and cataloging the books I brought back with me, wearing paper-thin muslins and fashionable silks is not exactly practical. Besides, Your Grace, I would rather not spend my money on fancy dresses I will rarely wear."

"Balderdash." The duchess plucked a lemon tart from the tea tray, took a bite, and chewed with obvious relish. "It has been well over a year since your husband's death, and you look like you're still in mourning for him."

"But I am not," Kit protested. "These are practical gowns, and appropriate for my station. After those gaudy creations that George wanted me to wear, I am relieved to have something more somber."

"Somber? You're a widow, child—you're not dead. Goodness, what harm will a few new frocks do?"

"I do not wish to be seen as . . . well . . . *fast,*" Kit insisted. "I will not make myself a target for any more impertinent remarks."

"Impertinent remarks?" repeated the duchess with a touch of outrage.

Kit opened her mouth, then closed it with a snap. She could not tell tales out of school, nor would she impugn the elderly woman's family as they had hers. The tips of her ears grew hot with the memory. "I do not wish to discuss it."

"Well, I am a widow, and no one questions *my* sense of propriety." The duchess cocked her head, her black eyes flashing, looking for all the world like an inquisitive bird. "I cannot believe you are so put off by wagging tongues. Gracious, I have never known you to be so missish!"

Heat bloomed in Kit's cheeks. She grimaced, then counted to five and took a deep breath. "I know you mean well, Your Grace," she stated at length, "but I will not allow you—or anyone else, for that matter—to push me at something I do not want."

The duchess's thin, lampblackened brows rose toward her hairline. "Well, perhaps not so missish, after all. Come now, child. You cannot expect me to believe that you actually enjoy racketing around this house by yourself, swathed in those shapeless sacks. If you were as desolated by that idiot's death as you would have me believe, you would have committed *suttee* like a poor Hindu widow."

The thought of throwing herself onto a blazing funeral pyre made Kit shudder. "Don't be ridiculous."

The duchess harrumphed. "Quite so. The time has come to form a strategy, my dear. Unless, of course, you intend to remain closed up in this house for the rest of your life."

"I have not given the matter much thought," Kit replied. Another knot of tension began at the back of her neck, but she resisted the urge to rub at it.

"Well, you should," prodded the duchess. Her severe

expression eased. "George Mallory may have been an insufferable popinjay, but I can see that he left you well provided for."

Kit blinked. "Yes—well enough. With all due respect, Your Grace, that is none of your business."

The dowager dusted crumbs from her fingertips and reached for a slice of Dundee cake. "I am making it my business, child. Such is the privilege of age and rank, especially for nosy old tabbies like myself who have little else to occupy their time. So . . . you mean to rest on your laurels? Fustian. You're too young to live like an . . . oh, what is that word again . . . an ascetic."

"I am five-and-twenty, Your Grace, once widowed, and possessed of only modest appearance, connections, and fortune. What would you have me do?" Kit shrugged and sipped her tea.

"Perhaps you need to take a lover," quipped the duchess over the rim of her teacup.

The young woman's gasp of shock sent a flood of liquid down her windpipe, and she began to cough. "*Really,* ma'am!" she sputtered. Her face a furious scarlet, she set her cup down with a clatter and fumbled for the kerchief she had tucked in her cuff.

The duchess gazed mildly back at her. "And why not? You are strikingly beautiful, despite your protests to the contrary. With a few alterations to your attire and your hair, I wager that handsome bucks would flock to your side by the score."

Kit started to lift a hand toward her tight chignon, then stopped herself. "Out of the question. I will be no man's mistress."

Mischief twinkled in the duchess's eyes. "Are you sure about that? Eh, I thought not. To tell the truth, you might be more prudent to find a husband."

Kit did not answer right away. "I am not certain I wish to be a wife, either," she declared. "I have been married once, and I do not care to repeat the experience."

"Why not?" The dowager finished the last bite of her Dundee cake, then eyed the plate of marzipan. "You're a woman who has seen something of the world, not some featherheaded chit just out of the schoolroom. This time you will be able to choose a proper husband."

Kit wagged a finger at her. "No, Your Grace."

The duchess pulled back, clearly affronted. "What do you mean, 'no'?"

"While I appreciate your concern, I wish to live my life *my* way. What man would countenance his wife spending all her time translating Hindu literature? I assure you that I am quite content the way I am."

The duchess drummed her fingers on the arm of the sofa. "I vow you delight in disobliging me."

Kit's smile melded with the rim of her cup as she sipped her tea. Lukewarm. Ugh. She made a face and set aside the cup. "The moment I decide to issue forth into society, Your Grace, you shall be the first one to know."

"Insolent, headstrong girl," muttered the dowager. "Very well, then. I shall say no more on the matter."

"May I have your word on that, ma'am?"

The duchess skewered her with a penetrating glare; Kit gazed back, unperturbed. After a few moments, Her Grace looked away.

"I suppose I am being rather high-handed with you," the older woman huffed. "All right. You have my word. 'Pon rep, you are a stubborn creature."

"Thank you, Your Grace." With a slight smile, Kit proffered the plate of marzipan.

The duchess waved it away. "No, thank you. You have quite ruined my appetite."

While she sipped her tea, the dowager went on to regale Kit with the latest news and gossip from London; the duchess seemed to find great amusement in watching young chits and their mothers scramble hither and thither like hens in a barnyard as they made their all-important preparations for balls and parties.

"Unfortunately, we will have no further diversions of that sort until autumn." Then the duchess paused and set down her teacup. "And now I have a favor to ask you."

Kit braced herself. "And that is? . . ."

"The last week of this month I am due to visit my grandson at his country estate near Stow-on-the-Wold. I had hoped you would consent to accompany me."

"Accompany you?" Kit pulled a face; she was doing it again. Soon she would be nothing but a complete mimic.

Her Grace did not appear to notice. "You make it sound like such a remarkable request, child. Really, I know of no other person whose company I can tolerate so well as yours."

Kit swiveled around in her chair and poured His Grace a fresh cup of tea, her shoulders hunched so that the duchess could not see her scowl. "How long will you be staying, ma'am?" she asked, trying to keep her voice steady.

"Oh, a week, at most. I would consider it a great favor to me, Kit. My great-grandchildren are delightful, but I fear my grandson and his wife are as stiff rumped as they come. They are convinced that I have become completely addled in my old age and that it is high time I settle down in the dower house and stop making a fool of myself. Bah. Stop making a fool of myself, indeed! I shall need your assistance in reasoning with these young idiots."

Kit pursed her lips. "I think it very wrong of them to force you to do anything, Your Grace."

"Yes, but that will not prevent them from trying, I can promise you that. But do not worry, child—you will have no social obligations and no responsibilities save to keep me from pulling caps with my relations. You will be there as my very great friend. Surely you agree that a change of scenery will do you good. Come with me, Kit, do."

The young woman considered the remaining liquid in the bottom of her cup. Spend a week in the home of the man who had tried to bribe her into severing her friendship with the dowager? The small fortune he had offered would have rendered her a very wealthy woman, but she did not hold her friends so meanly as His Grace did his own relations. Her jaw tightened. She had just gained her own freedom; she could not bear to see the dowager lose hers.

She raised her head. "If you believe my presence will help, then yes, Your Grace, I will go with you."

The duchess beamed. "Capital, my dear. Capital! It will be a week you will not soon forget."

Kit smiled back. "Oh, I am certain of it."

London

Bored.

Bored, bored, bored.

Nicholas Darcy, Marquess of Bainbridge, stifled a yawn with the back of one elegantly manicured hand. God's teeth, now that the Season was over, here he was, poised to cock up his toes from sheer *ennui*. Town was frightfully thin of company, and would be for the next two months. Nothing of note had been entered into the gaming book at White's, or any of the other gentlemen's clubs, for that matter. Recent bouts of inclement weather had kept him from his regular afternoon gallop. Even the lush blond charms of his mistress, the exquisite Angelique Auvray, were wearing thin; her fits of coquettish jealousy, which he had once found amusing, had become rather tedious of late. If he did not soon find something with which to divert himself, he would surely run mad.

At the moment, his only interesting prospect lay in a mysterious message from his cousin, the Duke of Wexcombe. The duke had written to him a few days ago, saying that he would be in London and needed to meet with the marquess on a most urgent matter. Bainbridge flicked a glance to the clock that ticked contentedly away on the marble mantelpiece. Nearly half past three. His cousin was due at any moment.

At precisely half past three, the marquess's lugubrious butler announced the arrival of His Grace, the Duke of Wexcombe. Lord Bainbridge climbed to his feet just as his cousin marched into the study.

"Good afternoon, Wexcombe," he drawled, making a slight bow. "I had never thought to see you in London after the close of the Season."

"I know," replied the duke, his face haggard. "But circumstances dictate otherwise."

Bainbridge looked hard at his relative, then arched a dark, quizzical brow. "Gadzooks, my dear fellow—something must be very wrong, indeed. You look as though you need a drink."

His Grace nodded and lowered himself into one of the two high backed plush chairs that flanked the hearth. "Yes, I believe I do. Brandy, if you please."

Well, well—this *was* a curious development; the stiff and proper Duke of Wexcombe rarely indulged in spirits, and never before dinner. But, ever the obliging host, Bainbridge crossed to the sideboard, uncorked the decanter, and poured two bumpers full of amber liquid. He handed one to his guest.

"I assume your rather unsmiling demeanor has something to do with your message," he prompted, settling himself into the chair opposite his guest.

The duke stared into the depths of his brandy, then regarded his cousin with somber gray eyes. "It involves my grandmother."

"Ah." Bainbridge settled back in his seat and savored a sip of his drink. "What is Great-Aunt Josephine up to now? Another adventure?"

His Grace made an impatient gesture. "She gets more difficult with every year," he grumbled. "At first I thought her odd starts were the result of boredom, but I vow she has become as eccentric as Lady Hester Stanhope herself. First her voyage to Greece, then to Turkey, then to India, of all places. And now . . ."

The marquess rubbed at his chin. Yes, his cousin could be a pompous ass. Yes, he was damnably high in the instep. But there could be no doubt that he loved his grandmother and cared for her welfare. Whatever had happened, it was something that did not bode well.

"And now?" he prompted.

The duke thrust a hand through his wheat-blond hair, undoing the careful Brutus style. "I feared this might happen. I shall be blunt, Bainbridge. Grandmama is no longer in complete possession of her faculties. *Non compos mentis.*"

The marquess frowned. "How can that be? I saw her a year ago Christmastide and she appeared right as rain."

His Grace sipped his brandy. "I believe she is in good physical health," he admitted, "but her judgment is not as it should be. Look at the company she keeps these days . . . that scandalous fellow, the poet—what's his name . . .

Shelley, and Lady Holland's Whiggish set. And then there was that balloon ascension, and now—"

"Just what are you saying, Wexcombe?" Bainbridge demanded. His cousin's words struck a chord of alarm.

The duke's mouth thinned. "A scurrilous personage has attached herself to Grandmama, no doubt with the hope of sponging off her, or even inheriting some of her fortune."

"A fortune hunter? Whatever gives you that idea?"

"When Grandmama returned from India, all she could talk about was a certain Mrs. Mallory, a widow she had met during the voyage. She spends more of her time with this woman than she does with her blood relations. I tell you, Bainbridge, it's not natural."

"A widow," the marquess mused. "Do you know anything about her? Perhaps she is just someone who befriended Aunt Josephine onboard ship. What exactly has you so concerned?"

His Grace took a long pull of brandy, then made a face. "I did some checking up on this woman, and you will like what I found even less than I did. She is the daughter of Baron Sudbrooke."

"Good God."

"My thoughts exactly. And it gets worse. Eight years ago she married a Cit by the name of George Mallory. A very wealthy Cit. Wealthy enough to pay off Sudbrooke's debts."

"His debts at the time, you mean," Bainbridge snorted. "Lud, the man's a sieve when it comes to money. Hasn't a feather to fly with."

"Quite."

"Didn't he flee the country last year?"

"Yes, and went to ground somewhere. His debts were excessive."

"So what are you worried about? If this Mrs. Mallory is a Cit's widow, she should have enough blunt of her own."

"On further investigation, I discovered that her jointure was relatively small." His lips twitched. "She has enough to live comfortably, but hardly in the manner to which I'm sure she has become accustomed. Like father, like daughter, I'll wager. Then just a few days ago I received a note from Grandmama, saying that she's bringing this woman with her to visit us in Gloucestershire."

Bainbridge considered this. "So you think this widow is planning to get her hands on Her Grace's money?"

"I do," replied the duke with a curt nod. "Grandmama will be seventy-four come Michaelmas. She is no longer as agile, physically or mentally, as she would like us to think, and therefore she is vulnerable. I think this Mrs. Mallory is egging her on, taking advantage of her lessened mental capacities."

A muscle flexed in the marquess's jaw. "Then we must look after her, Wexcombe."

"I am relieved to hear you say that, Cousin, because I came here to secure your help." His Grace leaned forward, his elbows resting on his knees and an intent, angry light in his eyes.

"What would you like me to do?"

A slight flush colored the duke's pale cheeks. "I pray you do not take offense at this, Cousin, but I believe we have need of your particular . . . talents."

"Ah. Do I take you to mean that you want me to seduce this Mrs. Mallory?" Bainbridge grinned in spite of himself.

"Anything it takes," the duke declared. The pink in his face grew brighter. "I've already offered her ten thousand pounds to leave Grandmama alone, but the jade refused it. She's probably holding out for a greater offer. See what you can do; I will pay whatever it takes. Seduce her, then abandon her if you have to. Just enough to give my grandmother such a disgust of this woman that she'll never want any further contact with her."

"Hmm. Won't this widow be suspicious? After all, my reputation often precedes me."

Wexcombe swirled the brandy in his glass, then shrugged. "You are my cousin, and this is a family house party. What is there to suspect?"

"What about the duchess and the children? I'm not sure how much of this sordid affair we will be able to hide from them."

"Caroline is aware of the situation, as is her sister Elizabeth, and I will instruct the governess to keep Nathaniel and Emma in the nursery. This might be our only opportunity, Bainbridge. Once the *ton* returns to Town, who knows what Grandmama might try to do? Lord knows I don't want a scandal on my hands."

The marquess snorted. He knew better than to think his cousin was doing this purely for his grandmother's benefit. But the dowager's welfare was at stake, so he could hardly refuse. "When do you need me at Broadwell Manor, Cousin?"

His Grace set aside his glass. "Grandmama and her . . . friend . . . are due to arrive next Monday; I would like for you to be there when they do."

"Then I shall pack at once and travel to Gloucestershire directly," Bainbridge stated. He rose and offered his hand to the duke. "After next week you shall have nothing to worry about."

Wexcombe took his hand and shook it gratefully. "I am counting on it."

"Just be careful. Remember what happened the last

time you tried to tell Great-Aunt Josephine what she should and should not do—she boarded the next ship for Calcutta."

The duke rolled his eyes. "You needn't remind me," he admonished, then took his leave.

Bainbridge stared after him. A slight smile crooked one corner of his mouth. How ironic. A few moments ago, he had wanted nothing more than something, anything to ease his crushing boredom.

He should really be more careful about what he wished for.

Chapter Two

*T*hey were staring at her.

Every time Kit raised her head from her book she fancied that she saw one of the others look quickly away. Or was she imagining things? The Marquess of Bainbridge, at least, made no attempt to conceal his scrutiny. The first time their eyes met across the drawing room, his lips curved in a slight, intimate smile that sent gooseflesh racing over her skin. A bright display of color rose in her cheeks, and Kit wrenched her attention back to her reading, though the words on the page made little sense to her restless mind.

She had expected some condescension from the relations of the dowager duchess, but not such veiled hostility. During dinner, the duke and duchess asked her a number of pointed questions about her experiences in India, but their inquiry seemed to focus more on her late husband's dealings in trade than on anything to do with Calcutta or its many wonders. Lady Elizabeth Peverell, the duchess's sister, had sat next to her, and although on the surface her conversation sounded quite congenial, the lady made several insulting comments *sotto voce* to her, well out of the dowager's hearing. Kit frowned. And this was but the first battle.

She shifted on the Chippendale chair and tried to concentrate on her book, but Mr. Coleridge's sonnets had lost their appeal. She had never traveled in such exalted social circles, even when she made her debut; the penniless daughter of a reprobate baron received few invitations, never mind vouchers for Almack's. Perhaps that was why she felt so out of place.

It had started the moment she and the dowager had arrived. Although Kit had worn her best gown to dinner, the sight of the lovely raven-haired duchess in her dress of celestial blue silk and Lady Elizabeth in a creation of silver net over sea green satin was enough to make her compare herself to a crow that had inadvertently landed in a flock of graceful swans. Her navy blue gown, though well made, looked woefully plain by comparison. Now she knew why the dowager duchess had gone on about new dresses. Kit pursed her lips and turned another page.

Since they dined *en famille*, the gentlemen did not go to a separate room to enjoy their port after dinner, but rather the entire group had adjourned to the drawing room. At present, the duke and duchess sat on either side of the dowager on the long striped divan by the hearth. The marquess lounged against the ornate stone mantelpiece, a glass of sherry dangling from his strong fingers. Lady Elizabeth sat nearby and attempted to engage the marquess in conversation. Lord Bainbridge, however, did not appear to be drawn in by her sallies; he made but brief replies, his gaze never straying far from Kit's.

What part did this fellow play in the duke's scheme? Whatever it was, she was determined not to let him unnerve her. With a huff, Kit turned a deliberate shoulder to him.

There, that was better. She tried to find her place in her book.

Was he still . . .

Temptation got the better of her. She glanced over her shoulder.

Yes, he was.

Heat flooded her features for the umpteenth time that evening. Why did the man stare at her so, and why did it seem to affect her pulse so strangely? He was handsome, very handsome, but something about his demeanor disturbed her, and it was not just the fact that he felt inclined to stare at complete strangers. He had—there was no other way to put it—an almost *deliberate* charm about him, as though he went out of his way to bring himself to the attention of the fairer sex. And he paid almost no attention to Lady Elizabeth, the lovely unmarried daughter of an earl, in favor of her, a plain-featured widow.

As if her experience on the Marriage Mart had not been education enough, Kit's experiences in India had honed her ability to identify dangerous predators, and this man was definitely dangerous. She could see it in the confident set of his broad shoulders, in the calculated smile that curved his mobile mouth. He continued to regard her from beneath seductively half-lowered lids; she dared not look into those compelling sable brown eyes, or imagine brushing that lock of ebony hair away from his forehead. . . .

She started. Gracious—what made her think such a thing? She had dealt with over a dozen such men in India, acquaintances of her husband who had not scrupled to solicit her affections, so why did this one have her behaving like a complete widgeon?

"Mrs. Mallory," called the duchess, "perhaps you would favor us with a piece on the pianoforte. I think you will find our Broadwood grand to be a superior instrument."

Kit now raised her head to find herself the focus of everyone's gaze. Again. She forced a polite smile to her lips. "I regret to say, ma'am, that my musical talents are indifferent, at best."

"Well then, I will play, and you can sing for us."

Kit recognized the gleam in the duchess's cool eyes. A prickling sensation spread across the back of her neck. "I fear my singing is little better, Your Grace."

"Oh, leave the girl alone, Caroline," reproached the dowager. "She is here as my guest and should not feel obliged to entertain you."

The duchess lifted a languid hand to her throat. "I was merely being polite, Grandmama. After all, we do want Mrs. Mallory to feel at home here." She turned to her husband. "Do we not, my dear?"

"Yes. Of course," agreed the duke, his mouth set in hard lines.

Kit's fingers tightened around her book. Did the dowager not notice the treacherous undercurrents of these words? Apparently not. That, or she was going to pick her battles. Kit hoped it was the latter.

"I confess I am astonished, Mrs. Mallory," added Lady Elizabeth. She shared a knowing look with her sister. "I thought every well-brought-up young lady knew how to play the pianoforte and sing. Your talents must lie in . . . other areas."

Kit's smiled turned brittle. "Quite so. I speak French and Italian tolerably well, although my German is only adequate. During my years in India I learned to speak fluent Hindi, along with a smattering of Bengali and a bit of Persian."

Lady Elizabeth appeared taken aback. "I . . . see. And

your other accomplishments? Do you embroider or paint watercolors?"

"I have always wondered why society insists on measuring a lady by her accomplishments. If playing and singing and painting insipid watercolors are the sum of our potential, then we are dull creatures, indeed."

"I must protest, Mrs. Mallory," said the duchess airily. "Such refined skills are what separate genteel ladies from women of the lower classes."

"One might also claim that the ability to read serves the same purpose." Kit gestured to her book.

"Oho—a palpable hit. Good for you, child," cackled the dowager.

Kit smiled. The lady was indeed picking her battles.

The duke scowled.

The marquess cleared his throat, and Kit would swear that he was trying to hide a grin of amusement.

"Do you mean to tell us that you would prefer to be a bluestocking, rather than a proper lady?" Lady Elizabeth twittered.

"I do not understand why the two need be mutually exclusive," Kit responded. "And I have never considered myself as anything but proper."

Her Grace made a dismissive gesture. "I fail to see what use a lady has for the scholarly skills you espouse, Mrs. Mallory."

"Just as I fail to see why intelligence is deemed of lesser value than musical skill. Why may a woman be considered clever or witty, but no more than that? God, in His infinite wisdom, gave us each certain talents. Some of us were meant to play the piano, just as others were meant to study poetry and philosophy."

The duchess rose from the divan, her mouth pinched. "Well, if you ask me, all of that sounds rather . . . revolutionary. I declare, Mrs. Mallory, next you'll be telling us that you sympathize with the French! Come, Lizzie. I wish to play, and I will need you to turn the pages for me."

The two women crossed the room to the Broadwood grand, then sat down together on the bench in front of the keyboard and put their heads together in conversation. Pointedly ignoring Kit, the duke turned to the dowager with a question about her plans for the upcoming Season. And the marquess. . . . The marquess detached himself from the mantel, crossed the Aubusson carpet, and sat down on the chair next to Kit.

He leaned toward her, his eyes on the book in her hands. Kit detected a faint hint of his cologne, musk with a trace of citrus, mingled with cheroot smoke and the smell of warm skin. George had always applied Imperial water with a rather heavy hand, claiming that it drove away the mosquitoes, and as a result the scent had never much appealed to her. The marquess's particular combination, however, was completely and utterly masculine. She swallowed hard.

"And which one are you studying now, ma'am—poetry or philosophy?" he inquired.

"Ah . . . poetry, sir," she replied when she found her voice. "By Mr. Hartley Coleridge."

"Coleridge? I do not believe I have heard his work. Would you consent to read some to me?"

His eyes were the color of chocolate, rich and dark. Strange, but never before had she found dark eyes so attractive.

"I would not think you a lover of poetry, my lord," she said, surreptitiously rubbing one damp palm against her skirts.

"You would be surprised at the things I find appealing," he murmured.

His devilish grin made Kit's heart give a strange, sideways leap. She glanced toward the pianoforte; the duchess had just launched into a spirited rendition of Mozart's "Rondo Alla Turca."

"I do not think it would be polite to ignore Her Grace's performance," she replied a trifle breathlessly.

A pained expression crossed the marquess's face. "I have always thought Caroline's technique to be somewhat . . . ah . . . energetic. She doesn't play the pianoforte so much as bang on it."

Kit bit her lip to stifle a sudden surge of laughter. "I am certain she would not appreciate your rather candid criticism, my lord."

He chuckled. "Then we shall have to keep it a secret, shan't we?"

That throaty laugh sent a shiver of pleasure down Kit's spine. She tried to ignore it. "I have never been one for secrets, sir."

"Oh, you are a cruel creature, Mrs. Mallory. I will be undone, and Caro will have my head!"

"I doubt that very much, for I will not be the one to tell her."

Lord Bainbridge raised a speculative eyebrow. "Will you give me your word on that?"

The corners of her mouth twitched. "You sound as though you do not trust me, Lord Bainbridge."

He extended a hand. "Here—let us shake on the matter. You agree to keep my secrets, and I shall keep yours. Oh, come now, ma'am. My reputation with my cousin is in jeopardy. I must know that you will keep my confidence."

She stared at his hand, at the broad palm and long fingers. "But I have no secrets, sir."

"No secrets?" He gazed back in mock disbelief. "Remarkable. Well, if you ever do, I promise that I shall keep them as close as a miser keeps his purse."

The teasing twinkle in his dark eyes proved too much; she smiled and took his hand. "Done."

His fingers closed over hers. The sensation of his warm, calloused skin around hers robbed her of breath. Effervescent fire raced through her veins. Her skin tingled. God in heaven—what was the matter with her?

The marquess held her hand for several heartbeats and showed no sign of wanting to release it. Then he turned her hand over, and his thumb caressed her palm.

Kit pulled her hand away. "You are too forward, sir."

"I am, aren't I?" Again, the roguish smile. "I have been told that it is one of my most endearing qualities."

Kit's smile dwindled as her conscience pricked her. The marquess was flirting with her, and making a concentrated effort to do so. Oh, the banter between them seemed natural enough, but he assumed a familiarity with her that set off warning bells in her head.

"Not to me, my lord," she reproached him. "If this is some sort of lark . . ."

Bainbridge smothered a sigh. This might be more difficult than he had anticipated. She was a cautious creature; his overt physical lures had not produced the results for which he'd hoped. This was the first widow he'd ever encountered who had *not* been eager for his touch. Time to adjust his strategy.

"Forgive me," he said with all the contrition at his command. "I did not mean to offend you. If I agree to behave myself, would you still consent to read aloud?"

"Behave yourself?" she asked archly. "Pray excuse my

blunt speech, my lord, but I am beginning to doubt if you are interested in poetry at all."

Careful.

He shrugged and spread his hands. "Ah. . . . You have found me out, Mrs. Mallory. I do have an ulterior motive."

Her green eyes narrowed. "And what would that be?"

Bainbridge shot a quick glance in the duke's direction. "My family, unfortunately, possesses much of the arrogance that often accompanies great rank," he murmured. "Truth be told, I think Wexcombe was born looking down that patrician nose of his."

She ducked her head, but not before Bainbridge spied her grin of amusement. "He is a duke, after all. I suppose he is entitled to a certain amount of pride."

"Entitled or not, I am rather ashamed of the way they have treated you this evening. I simply hoped to put you at ease and prove that not all of us have forgotten how to be civil."

"Oh," she replied, her fingers laced in her lap. Clearly, she had not expected him to say that. "And why have you taken this upon yourself, my lord? You do not share their estimate of my character?"

"The duke may be my cousin," he said with a lopsided grin, "but he does not make up my mind for me. My Great-Aunt Josephine—the dowager duchess—obviously holds you in great regard."

"Thank you." The tense set of her shoulders eased. "Might I ask you one other question?"

"As long as it does not involve poetry or philosophy," he chuckled, "for I was an indifferent student at best."

This time she responded to his jest with a genuine smile. "No, it involves neither. I merely wished to know you why you were staring at me."

"Was I staring?" he asked, feigning innocence. He had not put her off her guard, after all. Blast.

"You were," she countered. "And I cannot imagine why."

"Can you not?" Bainbridge willed her to meet his gaze, but she did not oblige him. He had to content himself with the study of her profile. "Surely you realize that you are a very attractive woman, Mrs. Mallory."

She blushed a vivid pink, and he spied the rapid flutter of her pulse at the base of her throat, in the soft hollow barely visible above the collar of her dark blue gown. He had told her the truth; she was attractive, in a very out-of-the-ordinary sort of way, and would be even more so if she wore more flattering colors.

No English rose, this woman. Her thick hair, scraped into a ruthlessly tight bun at the back of her head, gleamed a rich tawny gold in the candlelight. A few cinnamon-colored freckles dusted the bridge of her nose and the high-arched planes of her cheekbones. Her jaw was too square and determined for his taste, but her rosy mouth would tempt even a monk to madness. He might actually enjoy this.

"I think, my lord, that it might be more prudent to limit our discussion to poetry." Blushing, her eyes downcast, Mrs. Mallory ran a finger down the cover of the slender volume.

His lips quirked. "Indeed. For, despite my best intentions, I am still a scoundrel."

The duchess finished her performance with a flourish and a final chord, which was greeted with polite applause. She lanced a triumphant smile in Mrs. Mallory's direction, then started to select another piece from her sheaf of music. Bainbridge gripped the arm of his chair. So much for subtlety! If Caro continued in this provoking manner, the dowager duchess would demand to know the reason for their rudeness. And she would not like the answer.

But the dowager had paid no attention; she stifled yawn. "If everyone will excuse me, I will take this opportunity to retire. Good evening."

"Good evening, my lord." Mrs. Mallory rose from her chair in one graceful movement.

Bainbridge climbed to his feet. "You're not retiring as well, are you?" he protested. "It is early yet."

"I think it best," she murmured. Then, to the dowager, she declared, "I will accompany you upstairs, Your Grace. I find I am rather fatigued from our journey and also wish to retire."

The dowager nodded. "Come then, child, and let me lean on you. The evening chill makes my joints ache."

The duke sprang to assist her. "Let me help you, Grandmama."

"Nonsense," snorted the dowager as she levered herself from her seat. "Kit is perfectly capable of assisting me." The elderly woman held out her arm.

Mrs. Mallory dipped a curtsy to the room, then went to the dowager and allowed the older lady to lean on her as they proceeded into the hall.

"And to think we have to spend a full week in the company of that outrageous creature," huffed the duchess from the pianoforte. " 'Tis monstrous intolerable. And did you *see* that . . . that Hindu creature she brought with her? I tell you, Wexcombe, I do not want that heathen under my roof for any longer than is absolutely necessary."

"Rest assured, Caroline: we shall deal with Mrs. Mallory," the duke grumbled. "But in the meantime, you must restrain your displays of temper. Grandmama will suspect something is amiss if you are constantly baiting her guest."

"If you say so, my dear. But after tonight you cannot expect me to tip over the butter boat on her behalf," the duchess replied, wrinkling her *retroussé* nose.

"You will be polite," Wexcombe insisted. "We must not lower ourselves to her level."

"Very well. If I must," Her Grace muttered, then turned to the keyboard and attacked the opening measures of a Bach prelude.

The marquess ambled back to the mantel and retrieved his glass of sherry.

"Well?" His Grace queried. "How did you fare?"

"I thought I made some progress," the marquess replied, "but this widow is quite a slyboots. I'm not exactly sure what she's about. It may take some time to find out."

"We have only a week," the duke said with an exasperated sigh. "After that, we might never be able to pry her loose. Did you see how Grandmama has already come to depend upon her? Damnation—it curls my liver."

"Patience," counseled the marquess. "I will pierce her defenses soon enough. You may depend upon it."

"Are you so certain you can succeed?"

"Yes," Bainbridge murmured into his glass. "Just leave everything to me."

"So, what do you think of my family, child?" asked the dowager as they slowly ascended the sweeping marble staircase.

Kit pulled a face. What could she say that was not insulting? "I do not think they approve of me very much, ma'am."

"Do you require their approval?"

"No. You know I do not. "

The dowager chuckled. "Good. I thought as much. I tend to pay no attention to their hoity-toity ways. That, or I am so used to it after all these years."

"I wonder that you are able to tolerate it at all, Your Grace."

"Tolerate what? My dear girl, tonight they were on their best behavior," the dowager chortled.

Despite her best efforts, Kit could not restrain her sudden fit of giggles.

"I must say you held your own well enough against those fribbles," the elderly woman continued. "And speaking of which—what is your opinion of my great-nephew, Lord Bainbridge?"

Kit avoided the dowager's forthright stare. "Why do you ask, Your Grace?"

"Well, the two of you seemed to be having quite a coze just now."

"We . . . we were discussing poetry," Kit replied, hoping the shadows in the hallway would prevent the dowager from noticing the wave of embarrassed color that swept her face from jaw to hairline.

"Poetry?" Surprise tinged the dowager's tone. "I would never have thought a man like that would claim an interest in poetry. Racing and gambling, yes, but never poetry."

"A man like what?"

"Do not let his easy manner fool you, my dear. The marquess is a rake, a scoundrel who leaves nothing but broken hearts in his wake. He has quite a reputation in

London, you know. You would do well to be on your guard around him."

A rake? The word reverberated in Kit's ears. Well, that would explain his calculated flirtation. Or would it? Why would such a man even bother with her? She was a drab little wren when compared with the ethereal Lady Elizabeth, and yet he had called her attractive. Was his kindness to her an act? A prelude to seduction? Perhaps, yet his concern had seemed so sincere. Kit worried her lower lip between her teeth. What was she supposed to believe?

The rational side of her intellect warned her to avoid him. The irrational side was attracted to him, and infinitely intrigued. The marquess was amiable, handsome, and witty—everything George was not. Forbidden fruit, indeed.

The dowager patted Kit's arm with one wrinkled, blue-veined hand. "My great-nephew can be quite charming, but rakes never make good husbands."

"Good husbands?" Kit echoed. Then she sighed. She really must put a stop to that.

"No, not at all. Until they've been properly tamed, that is."

Kit's brows knit together. "What are you up to, Your Grace?"

"Why, nothing, child. I only thought to give you some good advice."

"Well, you need not concern yourself overmuch, ma'am, for I have no intention of marrying the marquess, or anyone else, for that matter!"

"I am glad to hear it. Perhaps now you can tell me about what else has been troubling you."

"Troubling—?" Kit caught herself just in time.

The dowager nodded, and the ever-present ostrich

plumes in her headdress nodded with her. "Quite. You've been cross as crabs ever since we left Bath."

Kit swallowed. "I have not," she lied.

"Really?" drawled the dowager duchess. "You forget how well I know you, my dear."

"It is a matter of little consequence," the young woman insisted. Her argument was with the duke, and the duke alone. Although she loved the older woman dearly, she did not want the dowager to fight her battles for her.

The duchess was not convinced. "Oh?"

Coldness washed over Kit. The dowager's perceptiveness threatened her resolve; the more she had to deceive the duchess, the less she liked it. "Nothing I cannot deal with upon our return, I assure you. And I apologize for being so out of temper."

The dowager peered intently at Kit. "I am willing to listen, child, if you wish to talk about it."

"Thank you, Your Grace," Kit replied with a wan smile, "but it's really not necessary."

When they arrived at the dowager's bedchamber, the elderly woman hesitated in the open doorway. She gave Kit's fingers a gentle squeeze. "If you need help, my dear, or assistance of any kind, you know you can always come to me."

"I appreciate your generosity, ma'am, but everything will turn up trumps," Kit answered. Then, in a whisper, she added, "I hope."

Chapter Three

The next day dawned fair and warm, and the duchess's suggestion of a drive to Stow-on-the-Wold garnered great enthusiasm from everyone but Kit, who pleaded a megrim and asked to remain behind.

"Are you certain, child?" asked the dowager, peering intently at her.

"I shall be fine, ma'am," Kit hastened to assure her. "It will pass. I just need to rest for a while."

"You do look a trifle fagged. Perhaps Lady Elizabeth should stay behind and sit with you," the dowager suggested.

The thought of spending time alone with the duchess's spiteful sister made Kit's abused temples throb all the more. And judging from the distasteful expression on her face, Lady Elizabeth welcomed the proposal no more than she did.

" 'Tis only a megrim," she replied before the elderly woman could become too fond of the idea. "Lakshmi can look after me. I would not wish to deprive any of you of this lovely weather."

"Well, all right," the dowager agreed, obviously reluctant. "We shall not be gone long, and I shall check on you when we return."

Kit watched from the doorway as the ladies climbed into the open carriage and the gentlemen mounted their horses.

Lord Bainbridge nudged his steel gray gelding close to her; he tipped his hat and favored her with a slight smile. "I do hope you will be well enough to join us for dinner. I am counting on you to rescue me from another of Caro's attempts on the pianoforte."

In his forest green jacket and buckskin breeches that hugged every curve of his muscular legs, the sight of him robbed Kit of breath. "I shall try, my lord," she managed at length, "but I make no guarantees."

He threw a brief glance over his shoulder at the duchess, who was holding down her fancy plumed bonnet against the assault of the mischievous breeze. "Then I shall pray for your immediate recovery," he drawled, and winked at her.

Kit gaped at him, but before she could form a reply the marquess replaced his curly-brimmed beaver atop his head and took up the reins. Then, in a clatter of hooves and crunch of gravel, the group was off down the driveway, trailing dust in their wake.

She watched them depart, one hand lifted in farewell, before pulling her paisley wool shawl closer about her shoulders and going back into the house.

The young woman wandered down the main hallway, absorbed in thought. Her headache was real enough, but more than anything she wanted solitude. A walk out-of-doors would give her an opportunity to make some sense of her disordered thoughts. She headed toward the back of the house.

Her temples continued to throb with a dull, steady

ache, as they had ever since she'd awakened. What a wretched night—nothing but hours spent lying awake staring at the pleated damask canopy above her bed, interspersed with short bouts of uneasy sleep. Even though she had drifted off eventually, she had not been asleep for very long before Lakshmi came to wake her.

She glimpsed her reflection as she passed by a wall-mounted mirror. Her dark blond brows formed a forbidding line across her furrowed forehead, and lines of anger and annoyance pulled at her mouth. Add to that the dark smudges under her eyes from lack of sleep, and she looked as awful as she felt. She made a face at her mirror self, then continued on, her arms wrapped around her body, her fingers clenched in her shawl.

The duke had refused to see her this morning. She had tried to speak to him before breakfast, but he had only glared down his aquiline nose and declared himself too busy at the moment to deal with her. When Kit persisted, His Grace snidely suggested that she make an appointment with his secretary, then turned on his heel and walked away.

She ground her teeth together. Some of the English nobles in Calcutta had condescended to her—and she had expected as much from them, given her husband's situation—but never had she been treated in such a rude and demeaning manner as she had this morning. Kit thrust open the French doors in the drawing room and crossed the slate-tiled patio in determined strides. She marched down the steps, through the garden, and past the manicured boxwood hedge before she realized that she had no idea where she was going.

Summer sunlight fell on her face and shoulders, and she tilted her head to meet its welcome warmth. Shielding her eyes against the brightness, she paused to survey her surroundings. She stood at the top of a gentle hill; below her, separated by a broad expanse of lawn, lay a man-made lake, sun-scattered diamonds winking on its rippled surface. A Grecian-style folly, complete with Ionic columns and a domed rotunda, presided over the shore on the far side. Beyond the lake, acres of field and forest flourished with verdant growth. Clouds of wooly sheep drifted through the rolling meadows. The brisk breeze, redolent with the odors of manure and freshly turned earth, blew a lock of loosened hair into her eyes.

She sat down on the grass, her legs folded beneath her. In this bucolic setting, the smells and noise and riot of color that was Calcutta seemed particularly far away. Her heart twisted. If George had not gone and gotten himself killed on that tiger hunt, she would still be there. At home.

Home. The word evoked the rustle of the breeze through the coconut trees, the patter of the monsoon rains on the roof, and the heavy, intoxicating scent of cape jasmine, the white flower that the Hindus called "*gandharaj.*" Happy memories, despite the farce that was her marriage. Her recollections of England were far less pleasant, but she would make new ones.

From across the lake drifted the sound of children's voices. Kit watched two figures, a girl and a small boy, come galloping out of the folly and along the shore of the lake on what looked like wooden stick horses. Behind them, a plump, soberly dressed woman followed at a more sedate pace.

Kit lifted a hand against the sun's glare as the two children approached, whooping and laughing. The girl appeared to be about five, with dusky curls drawn up in a blue ribbon that matched the sash of her muslin dress. The boy, whom Kit guessed to be a year or so younger than his sister, had tousled golden brown hair. His chubby features resembled the duke's, but there ended any similarity. Grass stains smudged the knees of his trousers, and somewhere along the line he had lost a button from his jacket.

The dowager had mentioned her great-grandchildren, but Kit had yet to meet them. She could not resist; she climbed to her feet. She made her way down the hill, waving to them as they approached.

"Hello!" she called. "What a fine day for a race! Won't you come and show me your ponies?"

The boy and girl saw her and slowed to a walk. The laughter left their faces; the little boy retreated behind his sister as Kit drew near.

"Hello," Kit repeated, giving them her best smile. She knelt down so her head was level with theirs. "What is your name?"

"I'm Emma," announced the girl, her gray eyes narrowed with suspicion. "Are you the bad lady?"

Kit blinked. "What do you mean?"

"Mama told Miss Pym to keep us away from the bad lady who was coming to visit. Well, are you?"

A chill coursed through Kit. Why would the duchess say such a thing? And what exactly did she mean by it?

"No," she replied, "I'm not a bad lady. My name is Kit, and I like children very much."

The boy peered out from behind his sister. "I'm Nathaniel," he murmured, his eyes huge.

"Hello, Nathaniel. I am very glad to meet you and your sister."

Emma did not appear convinced; she continued to regard Kit with belligerent wariness. "Did you come from Perdition?" she demanded. "Mama said she wished you were back there. Is that in France?"

"No," Kit replied, swallowing her shock, "I do not believe it is. But I am not from Perdition; I come from India."

"India!" Emma gasped, and at once her features transformed from distrustful to awestruck. "Great-Grandmama has been to India, too! She told us all sorts of stories about tigers, and elephants, and monkeys, and . . . and . . ."

". . . and peacocks, and water buffalo, and sacred bulls with garlands of flowers on their horns?" Kit prompted.

The little girl beamed at her, eyes wide with wonder. "Yes!"

The governess caught up with them, blowing hard, her face red as though she'd been running. She cast a frantic look at Kit, then latched on to Nathaniel's hand. "Come, children. Time to go into the house." She reached out her other hand for Emma, but the girl pulled away.

"No! I want to hear a story about India. Kit has been there, too, just like Great-Grandmama."

Miss Pym's nostrils flared. "I will tell you a story when we return to the nursery."

Emma stamped her foot. "I want Kit to tell me a story about India!" she shrilled.

"I'm sure Mrs. Mallory is far too busy to tell you any stories today," insisted Miss Pym. She darted another nervous glance at Kit. "Now, come along."

Kit climbed slowly to her feet and brushed the grass from her skirt. Her shoulders drew taut. "It's all right, Emma. Perhaps I can tell you a story tomorrow."

"No, now!" the girl cried. "Please?"

"Emma, a young lady should never raise her voice," Kit instructed gently. "I'm sure there will be plenty of time for stories later."

"Well," began a flustered Miss Pym, "I'm not sure that—"

"Oh, come now, Miss Pym," came a roguish chuckle from behind them. "Surely you can manage to fit one story into the children's busy schedule."

Kit whirled. Lord Bainbridge strolled toward them, a jaunty grin on his face.

The governess swallowed hard, then bobbed a nervous curtsy to the marquess. "I will see what can be arranged," she replied, her lips flattened in a thin line. "Come inside Master Nathaniel, Lady Emma. *Now.*"

Emma allowed Miss Pym to snatch up her small hand. She turned pleading eyes to Kit. "Promise you'll tell us a story?"

"Promise?" echoed Nathaniel. He stared beseechingly at her, his lower lip a-quiver.

"I promise," Kit murmured, putting on her bravest face.

She watched in silent anger as the dumpling governess dragged the two reluctant children and their toys up the hill and into the house.

"I take it your headache is better?" Bainbridge inquired in an innocent tone.

Kit flushed. Actually, the throbbing had progressed from her temples to the base of her skull, but she was determined to ignore it. "Well enough," she replied stiffly. "What are *you* doing here, my lord? Making sure I don't run off with the silver?" She bit her lip; she hadn't meant for that last part to slip out.

The marquess's grin widened. "Not at all. The dowager duchess was worried about you and asked me if I would return to the house to keep you company."

"Why did she send you?" Kit wondered aloud.

"She thought you might look more favorably on my company than that of Lady Elizabeth."

"You are correct, my lord. Five minutes in that lady's company and we are at daggers drawn."

"I am unarmed, I assure you," he said, amusement dancing in his dark eyes. "May I escort you back up to the house?"

She looked up at the Palladian grandeur of Broadwell Manor, at the path so recently taken by the duke's two children. Her smile faded. "Tell me something, my lord—why would the duchess ask Miss Pym to keep the children away from me?"

"What?" The marquess's brow puckered. "Whatever gave you that idea?"

"Not 'what,' my lord—'who.' Emma asked me very distinctly if I was the bad lady about whom her mama had warned Miss Pym."

"Out of the mouths of babes," murmured Lord Bainbridge.

Kit continued to regard him with a steady, searching gaze. "What is going on here, sir? I suppose that pride and protectiveness may account for a portion of the Their Graces' behavior, but to think I would be an immoral influence on their children without even knowing who I am—that is ridiculous."

Bainbridge silently berated his sudden predicament; young Emma's unfailing honesty had left him in a devil of a bind. He decided to change the subject.

"Come take a turn around the lake with me," he said, proffering his arm.

She hesitated. "I do not think it wise that I be alone with you, sir."

She was a cautious creature, but he enjoyed a challenge. "The garden, then." When she hesitated, he added, "I assure you that we shall be in full sight of the house at all times."

Mrs. Mallory stared at him for a moment, her lower lip caught between her teeth in a very appealing manner; then she laid her hand upon his arm. Her touch, though very light, sent a jolt of awareness through his body. Her tawny hair and unusual eyes gave her a striking appearance; she did not conform to the standards of English beauty, yet he found her damnably attractive. He couldn't put his finger on an exact reason why, but he did nonetheless. She seemed quite slender, but as she walked up the hill with him, he thought he detected the suggestion of curves beneath her shapeless brown sack of a dress. Interesting.

"Her Grace's tales of India are legendary in this house," he remarked. "She has made Caro faint on more than one occasion."

Mrs. Mallory laughed, a delightful, throaty ripple. "I will have to ask Her Grace what produced such a reaction; perhaps I might be so fortunate."

"I am sure you have quite a few stories of your own. Did you live in India long?" he asked.

"Seven years," she replied.

He detected a note of wistfulness in her words. "You miss it."

She turned away. "Yes."

"And do you miss your husband?"

A flush stained her cheekbones, highlighting the freckles scattered across them. Her brilliant green eyes narrowed in reproach. "That is an impertinent question, sir."

"I specialize in impertinence, as you may have noticed. Last night at dinner I detected a note of unhappiness in your voice when you spoke about him." Jade. That was the color. Her eyes reminded him of Chinese jade.

She pursed her lips. "My husband and I had a marriage of convenience, sir."

"Ah . . . so you mean you do *not* miss him." He smiled.

She gasped and blushed a deeper shade of pink. "It is none of your business."

"Not that I blame you," he interjected. "He sounded like a rather dull fellow, a poor match for someone of your obvious wit and intelligence."

"Come now, my lord, none of your flummery." She tilted her head to look him in the eye. "Her Grace warned me about you, you know."

"Did she?" He quirked an eyebrow. "And just what did my great-aunt tell you?"

"That you were a rake and a scoundrel who left a trail of broken hearts in his wake."

His smile turned suggestive. "I do have that reputation."

"You sound rather proud of it."

"Why should I not be?"

"So you enjoy breaking hearts?" Her amazing eyes regarded him with undisguised interest.

"Do I?" The back of his neck grew hot. "That is a rather singular question, Mrs. Mallory."

"I do not see why you alone have license to be impertinent," she declared. "Well, do you?"

How quickly she had put him on the defensive. Thrust, parry, and riposte, indeed! "I don't think I've broken too many," he replied. "And certainly not on purpose."

"But if you know you might break your mistress's heart eventually, why do you do it?"

He blinked. "I beg your pardon?"

Her gaze did not waver. "Why do you do it?"

"You mean . . . why am I a rake?" he asked, incredulous. Ye Gods. No other Lady of Quality would dare ask him such a thing. "Do you always speak your mind, Mrs. Mallory?"

"I do when I think someone is evading my questions."

Touché! Bainbridge threw back his head and laughed. Lord, she intrigued him more with each passing moment! "Then I shall have to be honest with you, ma'am, or you will never let me hear the end of it. The truth of the matter is that I enjoy women—and sampling the different pleasures they have to offer."

The blush in her cheeks spread over her entire face. "I see."

"Most of the attraction is physical; surely you can understand that, having been married."

She ducked her head, and did not reply.

Ah . . . the demure little widow had gotten herself in over her head. He chuckled. "I admire long legs, a lovely neck, and a slender figure with a high, rounded bosom. Nothing too overblown. A figure, in fact, rather like yours."

Her eyes rounded in surprise. Then her lips flattened, and she started to pull away from him. "Really, my lord. You are doing it again."

"Never say I didn't warn you. But I'm not finished."

"That's quite all right. You have satisfied my curiosity."

"Oh, come now, Mrs. Mallory," he reproached her. "You wanted an honest answer, and I am attempting to give you one. Or are you afraid to hear it?"

She straightened, a rebellious set to her chin. "I am not. Pray continue."

He slowed to a halt and leaned closer to her, close enough to smell her perfume, an exotic blend of sandalwood and gardenia. "I was saying," he murmured, "that most of the attraction is physical, but not the entire focus of my interest."

"Is it not?" Her tongue darted out to moisten her lips.

"No." He brushed a stray lock of hair away from her eyes. She shivered at his touch. His groin tightened. "I also favor a woman with a ready wit and more than a modicum of intelligence. A woman who has seen something of life and knows what she wants. What do you want, Mrs. Mallory?"

She gave a visible swallow and looked up at him. "Then why not marry, my lord? Why not find a woman who attracts you on both points?"

He leaned closer still, until his mouth was inches from hers. "Now you are evading *my* question, so I'll ask you again: what do you want out of life? Really want?"

"I . . . I don't . . ."

Her rosy lips parted. That was all the invitation he needed.

He kissed her. Not a forceful kiss, for that would frighten her, but a gentle, teasing kiss designed to test her response, to draw her out. Or at least that was what he intended. She tipped her head back, her warm lips parted beneath his. Lord, she tasted good, like exotic spices and sunshine. Her sandalwood perfume enveloped him. Every nerve in his body flickered to life.

He shifted an arm around her waist; she trembled but did not resist. He pulled her to him, inordinately pleased to discover the narrow span that lurked beneath the acres of fabric she wore. A narrow waist, flaring hips, and more bosom than he would have imagined. Intoxicating. With a groan, he cupped her rounded bottom, pulling her hips against his.

She stiffened, gasped, then wrenched herself away from him, her cheeks scarlet, her eyes ablaze with green fire. Her fingers shook as she touched her swollen lips. "What I want, my lord," she spat, "is to live without fear of being seduced by an unprincipled rogue!" With that, she clutched her shawl around her shoulders and fled through the opening in the boxwood hedge.

The marquess stared after her, breathing hard, his erection pressing against the tight confines of his breeches. His blood sang through his veins. God, he wanted her. One kiss, and he wanted nothing more than to sheath himself within her, to claim her completely.

Madness! He was getting caught up in his own trap.

He shook his head, as if he'd just emerged from a dream, and exhaled in a long sigh. Never had he lost control of himself like that, save when he was a callow youth. What was the matter with him? Something about her response to his kiss had tempted him past the point of reason—and all he wanted right now was to kiss her again. He hadn't felt this great an attraction to a woman since . . . well . . . his current mistress. He grinned. At least he knew he hadn't lost his charm.

The marquess pulled out his pocket timepiece. The others would be back soon. At least he'd had time to put the first portion of his plan in motion, if not the most critical part. Resolving to seek out Mrs. Mallory later, he tugged at his rumpled jacket and started off in the direction of the house.

When his relations returned from their outing, the marquess found the duke surly, the duchess near tears, Lady Elizabeth petulant, and the dowager up in the boughs. Without so much as a glance left or right, her face pinched in a terrible scowl, the dowager started up the stairs to her room. The duke offered to assist her, but she waved him away. The duchess and her sister retreated to the drawing room and closed the door.

Bainbridge turned to his cousin. "What happened?"

"We tried to talk with her," Wexcombe replied with a growl. "Asked her to come and live in the dower house. Demmed stubborn woman won't see reason."

The marquess folded his arms over his chest. "You mean she won't accede to your demands. Devil take it, I told you—"

The duke cut him off. "I've had enough of this, Bainbridge! She should be at home with her family, not gadding about like a giddy schoolgirl."

"Wexcombe, you're about as subtle as a hammer to the head," the marquess said with a sigh. "You cannot use your rank and position to bully your own grandmother. Let me talk to her."

"I doubt you'll be able to do any better," snapped the duke. "You know what she's like once she has set her mind to something."

"I just hope you haven't made a mull of it. After all, you want to persuade her to enjoy your company, not escape it."

Wexcombe scowled. "I tried, Cousin, but I've never known anyone to be so willful."

"You haven't been going about it the right way. Persuasion is the key, not force. I'll see what I can do." With a nod to the duke, Bainbridge started up the stairs.

He knocked at the door to her room. "Great-Aunt Josephine? Are you in? It's Bainbridge."

The door opened a crack; the dowager's maid regarded him with distrustful eyes. "Her Grace is resting, my lord."

The marquess presented her with his most dazzling smile. "Please tell Her Grace that I would like to see her."

"A moment, my lord." The abigail closed the door.

A few heartbeats later, Bainbridge was ushered into the dowager duchess's sitting room. The dowager reclined on the chaise before the fireplace, a blanket over her knees. The marquess's heart sank. Lord, she looked so drawn, so tired, so . . . old. She stared into the fire, her complexion ashen.

"Hello, Aunt," he said softly.

Her dark gaze swiveled to his face. A spark of interest glittered there for a moment, then disappeared. She turned back to the fire. "Hmph. Are you here to take a turn at me, as well?"

"Not at all. May I sit down?"

The dowager made a vague gesture toward the Chippendale chair across the hearth from her; Bainbridge lowered himself into it and leaned forward, his elbows resting on his knees.

"Well, what is it, then?" the dowager asked, her wrinkled lips still pursed in a frown.

"I'm sorry, Aunt Jo," he said. "I had no idea they planned to do this."

"I should hope not," she snapped. "I should hate to have to disinherit you, as well."

"You don't want to do that. They meant well; truly they did."

The duchess rose to a sitting position, her eyes flashing. "Oh, they did, did they? Cow-handed idiots, the lot of them! Think they can put me out to pasture like some broken-down nag. Balderdash. I won't stand for it. This is my life, and I'll be damned if I let that popinjay grandson of mine dictate to me!"

A smile curled at the corner of Bainbridge's mouth. "None of your die-away airs now, ma'am," he drawled.

The dowager squinted at him, then guffawed. "Oh,

Nicholas, they have me in such a pet. Pour me a glass of brandy—for medicinal purposes, of course."

"Of course." With a grin, Bainbridge rose and crossed to the washstand, where the dowager kept a bottle of smuggled French brandy and a glass in the small cupboard beneath it. That he kept her provided with the contraband liquor was their secret; if smuggled brandy kept her happy, all the better. He poured a small amount into the glass, then handed it to her.

"You're a good lad, Nicholas," sighed the dowager. The rings on her fingers flashed in the firelight as she took a sip. "I am relieved to see that someone in the family inherited my intelligence."

He folded himself into his chair. "But I am only your great-nephew by marriage," he pointed out.

The dowager harrumphed. "Then that explains it. A pity one cannot choose one's blood relations." She peered at her glass, then at him. "And how is Kit?"

His pulse leaped at the mere mention of Mrs. Mallory's name. His pulse and . . . other portions of his anatomy. He shifted on his chair. "I believe she is much improved, ma'am."

"Good. What do you think of the girl?"

One corner of his mouth twitched. He was sure the dowager didn't want to hear his salacious thoughts. "Girl? She is a bit old to be called that, don't you think?"

"Oh, bosh. At my age, everyone younger than fifty is a mere babe. Besides, she's only five-and-twenty. Hardly long in the tooth."

He raised an eyebrow. "And why are you telling me this, ma'am?"

"Well, because I want your estimate of her character," she blustered.

"She seems a pleasant enough lady," he hedged. "Then

again, I must admit that I hardly know her." *Though I find myself particularly eager to make her most . . . intimate acquaintance.*

She took another sip of brandy, coughed, and fanned her face with her kerchief. "No, no, stay there; I am quite all right. I met her onboard the *Daphne*, bound from Calcutta. She nursed me through that most dreadful passage; most of the time I was ill with horrible bouts of *mal de mer*. Eh . . . I do not wish to remember it too closely.

"Kit is a delight, Nicholas, and not only because she sees me as a person, not as a doddering eccentric whose presence is to be tolerated. She treats me with respect and genuine affection, which is more than what I've received from my own family of late. Now, what do you think of that?"

"Such a friendship is commendable, Your Grace."

The dowager fixed him with a pointed stare. "Then why does no one else in this house seem to agree with you?"

"Your Grace?"

"Oh, come now, Bainbridge, it's as obvious as this beaky nose of mine. Do you think me blind as well as deaf?"

"Neither, ma'am," the marquess was quick to reply.

"Well, my grandson apparently does. And I think I know the reason."

"And what would that be?"

The dowager snorted. "They think she's after my money."

"And you do not?" he inquired with great caution.

"You must believe Wexcombe's absurd prating if you think me so dicked in the nob, Bainbridge. Kit is not after my money; her late husband left her flush in the pocket. Do you think I don't realize what all this is about? This sudden push to get me to give up my independence, and the reprehensible treatment of my young friend?"

"You cannot blame Their Graces for being concerned for your welfare," Bainbridge gently replied.

"Perhaps, but I will not let them ramrod me into giving up my independence. After forty years of marriage to a man I loathed, I am entitled to enjoy a measure of freedom, and I intend to do just that."

"But at what cost, ma'am? You will be seventy-four on your next birthday. You have to slow down eventually."

"Why? I feel right as rain. Oh, I get a little slower each year, I will agree, but other than that I am in prime twig." She set her glass on the end table and glowered at him. "Where do you stand in all this, Nicholas? No, do not bother to give me that innocent look. It won't fadge. You rarely come to these family house parties, and yet this year, here you are. Has my grandson enlisted you in this nefarious plot of his?"

"What plot is that?"

"Do not insult my intelligence, boy. He called you here to persuade me to retire to the dower house at Wexcombe Hall, and to stop embarrassing him."

He raised his hands in protest. "I do not ascribe to those motives, I assure you. But I do fear for your safety, ma'am. Despite your protests, you are not as spry as you used to be, yet you insist on racketing around the world without apparent care for your health or your welfare. At times I wonder if you are trying to prove something to us."

"I?" she blurted. "I am not trying to prove a thing. What an absurd notion."

"We only want what is best for you."

"What is best for me, Bainbridge," the dowager

sniffed, "is for all of you to trust my judgment. I will decide when to settle down, and that is that."

"You are uncommonly stubborn, Your Grace."

She shrugged. "I do not wish to hear another word on the matter from you, Nicholas. Do you understand?"

Wexcombe was right about one thing: when the dowager duchess got a notion into her head, trying to reason with her was like arguing with the wind—it went its own direction, no matter what you said. "Very well, Aunt Jo."

The dowager nodded, satisfied. "Good. Now pour yourself a glass of brandy, Nicholas, and tell me what other nasty surprises are in store for me this week."

Chapter Four

Kit set down her pen with an aggravated sigh and massaged her cramped fingers. So much for trying to distract herself. At this rate, she would never finish translating Tulsīdās's *Ramayana*. She stared at her handwriting, which was uncharacteristically halting and uneven and almost illegible, then at the smudges of ink on her fingertips. What a mess she'd made. Of everything.

Propping her chin on the heel of one hand, Kit stared morosely out the windows at the clouds gathering on the horizon until her vision blurred at the edges. Why had she goaded the marquess like that? How foolish of her to think that she could give a rake a disgust of her through plain speaking. She'd been playing with fire; she should not have been surprised when the marquess gave her that scorching kiss.

Her lips still tingled. She rubbed her mouth to dispel the sensation. Why her? Because she was a widow, a woman of experience? Kit snorted. *That* was a misnomer. George had been an indifferent husband; he had wanted a high-born wife who would lend credibility and panache to his business, and who would ornament his home. Ornament, indeed. She might as well have been one of the trophies mounted on the wall. When she protested, he had not cared a whit for her feelings. And he had been indifferent to her in their marital bed, as well. It was just as well that they'd never had children. Kit rubbed at the gooseflesh on her arms. For seven years she had convinced herself that she was undesirable, and now. . . .

The marquess had to be trifling with her. A family house party must seem quite dull to a Corinthian such as he, so he must be looking for a diversion. That was the only way she could explain that amazing kiss. She could still feel the insistent pressure of his mouth against hers, still smell his lingering scent on her skin. . . .

She shook herself. No. She must not be tempted by this forbidden fruit. She would not subject herself to another man's whims. First her father, then her husband—twice was quite enough, thank you very much.

Kit returned her pen to its stand, closed the cap on the inkwell, and rose from the escritoire. Conversation with the dowager would ease her mind. She gave her hair a quick pat, then left her bedchamber and made her way to Her Grace's rooms.

As she approached, the marquess emerged from the dowager's rooms and closed the door behind him. She came to an abrupt halt, turned, and was about to retreat back the way she'd come when his voice stopped her.

"Mrs. Mallory. I had not thought to see you again so soon."

Kit scowled at the teasing challenge in his voice. She swiveled to face him. "Good afternoon, my lord," she replied in clipped tones. "I shall not trouble you; I am on my way to see the dowager duchess."

"You are too late, I fear," he replied with a slight smile. "She has just retired for a brief rest."

"Oh." Kit tried not to let her disappointment show on

her face. "Then I shall not disturb her. If you will excuse me—"

"A moment." He drew near with long-legged strides. "I wish to speak with you."

Kit's shoulders stiffened. "If you wish to apologize, my lord, I am willing to listen. Otherwise, I must bid you good day."

"Apologize?" His smile broadened. "Why would I do that, when I am not sorry for a moment about what passed between us?"

She stared at him, her mouth rounded in a perfect *O*. "Why do you persist in mocking me?"

"I am not mocking you."

"Then why did you kiss me?"

"Because, my dear Mrs. Mallory, you need kissing. Passionately, thoroughly, and as often as possible."

"Of all the—!" she sputtered. "Impudent—"

"—insolent, impertinent, impolite . . . Rest assured, ma'am, I have heard the entire litany." An impatient expression erased his smile. "Now, will you kindly forgo your maidenly protestations and listen to me for a moment?"

Kit closed her mouth with a snap. If the marquess continued to bait her like this, she would sound like a Billingsgate fishwife before the end of the week. "Very well, my lord."

"Thank you." Raised voices rang from the vestibule: the duke and duchess. Lord Bainbridge gestured toward the other end of the hall. "Let us walk a while together; the gallery might afford us more privacy."

Kit's heart did a strange flip at the thought of being alone with him, but her head did not forget so easily. "No more of your games, my lord."

He spread his hands. "No games; you have my word.

I only wish to discuss the welfare of the dowager duchess."

Every instinct told her not to go, but the quiet concern in his voice overrode her better judgment. She flicked an alarmed glance to the dowager's door. "Is anything wrong?"

He shook his head. "Not at the moment, no. She is merely a trifle fatigued. That is, however, what I wish to discuss with you."

"Then you have my complete attention, sir."

The marquess clasped his hands behind his back and began to wander down the hall toward the gallery. Kit fell into step a few paces to one side.

"Apparently," began Lord Bainbridge, "the duke used today's outing as an opportunity to ask his grandmother to retire from society and move into the dower house at Wexcombe Hall. No, not ask. Demand. Such an approach did not sit well with Her Grace."

"No, I imagine not," Kit replied tightly. Her hands balled into fists at her sides. "She suspected that the duke might try something like this; she told me he has been after her for months. Did he upset her very much?"

The marquess shook his head. "She will recover, but she remains stubbornly opposed to the idea of giving up her adventures."

"Of course she does. She is hardly in her dotage, after all."

"But she is not getting any younger, either. And I know my cousin—he will keep at her until she consents."

"Why do you tell me this?" She shot him a distrustful look.

"Because my great-aunt considers you a friend. A very great friend. And I know she will listen to your counsel."

Kit held up a warning hand. "If you are thinking of

asking me to help you in this endeavor, I can tell you that I will have no part of it."

The marquess frowned. "I must beg you to reconsider. The dowager duchess is a formidable lady, but I worry for her. She seems determined to prove to everyone just how independent she is, and she will go to any length to do so."

"What makes you think that?" Kit demanded. They had reached the gallery, a long, wide hall that housed portraits of obscure ancestors dating back several centuries. Trying to ignore all the eyes that seemed to stare down at her from the walls, she halted, her hands on her hips. "If that is truly what you believe, then you are mistaken, my lord."

He cocked his head to one side. "Am I?"

She bit her lip. "I believe she behaves the way she does because she enjoys it. She wants to meet new people, travel to new places. Everything she was denied during her marriage to that stuffy old duke."

He folded his arms across his chest. "You appear to have learned a great deal about her during your lengthy acquaintance."

His sarcasm brought scalding heat to her cheeks. "On board ship, my lord, there is little to do but converse with one another and play chess to pass the time."

"For six months? A rather dull prospect."

"Not when one is speaking with the dowager duchess. She told me enough to know that we have much in common. Her only misfortune is that she was not widowed at an earlier age."

"You astound me, ma'am," he drawled, clearly amused. "No more of this roundaboutation; I pray you speak your mind."

She flushed. "What I am trying to say is that I have

never known anyone else with such *joie de vivre*," she continued. "Her Grace delights in life, my lord, despite her advanced years. Every day is a new adventure."

"But what happens when she overestimates her capacity for such adventure?" he argued.

"What makes you think she will?" Kit shot back. "I believe that is what troubles her most: her own family does not trust her to know what is best. No one seems to bother to talk to her at all, save to criticize her. How would you like it if your family were to think you nothing but an inconvenience?"

Bainbridge sighed and thrust a hand through his hair, leaving it tousled as though he'd just risen from bed. Kit's blush deepened at the thought.

"What makes you so fond of my great-aunt? Aside from her sense of adventure, that is. Forgive me, Mrs. Mallory, but the difference in your ages does not exactly lend itself to a sharing of common interests."

Kit sidestepped him to stare up at a gilt-edged painting. "She is the closest friend I have ever had."

"What, had you had none before you met her?" he asked.

She shook her head. "Not really. Passing acquaintances, of course, but no bosom bows. My mother died when I was young, and afterward my father and I lived a rather insular existence in Hertfordshire. Several years later, when I made my debut, I discovered that his less-than-sterling reputation had tarnished me, as well; I received few invitations, and fewer offers. When I married George and went to India, the peers there looked down their noses at me because I'd married a Cit, and the Cits' wives did not like me because they believed I held myself above them, and that given the chance I would treat them as rudely as everyone else of my class did."

Kit heard Bainbridge's soft footsteps on the carpet, coming closer.

"What about your family? Did no one welcome you back home?" he murmured.

He sounded like he was standing right behind her. She shivered. "No one, my lord."

"Not even your father?"

"I heard through my husband's solicitor that my father fled the country last year to escape his creditors. He never bothered with me after my marriage, and I have not kept in close contact with anyone else."

His hands gently grasped her shoulders. "I am sorry," he said simply.

"You need not be, my lord. Ever since Her Grace and I befriended each other, I have not been lonely." She eased away from his touch, then turned to face him. "But you must not think me selfish; I do not want to see Her Grace keep her independence just so I am guaranteed companionship. I would never think of her so meanly. I have spoken in her defense because I agree with her, and I want her to be happy."

"So do I, but my cousin can be ruthless when he's crossed, Mrs. Mallory," he stated. "I suspect that he will even withhold the children from her if she does not consent. He may have already threatened to do so."

"Oh, I pray he does not," she murmured. "That will only serve to make everyone miserable, especially Her Grace. You must help me, my lord. Help me convince the duke that he cannot rob his grandmother of her freedom. If she is not allowed to make her own decisions and live her own life, she will wither away to nothing."

"But I also do not want to see my great-aunt throw caution to the wind with these 'round the world escapades of hers. She must start to show some restraint."

He stood so close to her; her eyes were on a level with the sparkling diamond pin in his cravat. But strangely enough, she did not feel threatened. Rather, she found in his solid presence a source of strength. She stared up at him with beseeching eyes. "There must be some sort of middle ground, a compromise that will satisfy both the duke and his grandmother. His Grace will not listen to me, but he will listen to you. Lord Bainbridge, if you care for your aunt's welfare, then I beg you—for her sake—help me."

He regarded her intently for a moment, his dark eyes mere slits. A tic jumped at the corner of his jaw. "I will make you a bargain, then, madam," he replied, his voice rough and throaty. "If I help you to forge a compromise with the duke, then you must agree to become my mistress."

She stared back at him with enormous green eyes. "You cannot be serious."

"I am completely in earnest," he replied. His plan had been to gauge her sincerity and thereby learn more about her, but the more he thought about the premise, the more it excited him. Lord, standing this close and not touching her was sweet torture. All he had to do was reach out and pull her into his arms. . . . He gave himself a swift mental slap. None of that. He needed to focus on acting like a complete and utter scoundrel.

"You are despicable, sir," she breathed, a slight quaver in her voice.

"You knew what I was when you asked for my help," he pointed out.

Her agitated gaze flicked wildly around the room. "Why?" she demanded. "Why would you put such a condition on something so important?"

Bainbridge shrugged. "Your idea has merit, but you

will need my help. And my help comes at a price." Now he would see if she wanted what was best for the dowager, or if she had other motives.

Trembling, she retreated until she bumped into the wall. "How could you do this to me? To your aunt?"

The evident pain on her face gave him a twinge. "Do you find the idea of being my mistress so reprehensible?"

She swallowed. "I value my freedom, my lord, and my dignity. I am not a . . . a *thing*, to be used and discarded at your whim."

"I never said you were. This relationship would be mutually rewarding, Mrs. Mallory—Kit." A smile quirked the corner of his mouth. "How did you come by that pet name? I find it delightful."

"My mother," she said. "My given is Katherine, and when I was a little girl, I would curl up next to her on the sofa when she sewed, just like a kitten." Her gaze metamorphosed from frightened to wary. "Do not try to distract me, my lord. It won't work."

He resisted the impulse to chuckle. Time to up the ante. "Just so. Then as I was saying, such a relationship would be gratifying for both of us. You would still have your freedom; this agreement would simply allow us to enjoy each other's company, physically as well as intellectually. I can use my influence to open doors for you, to further your own interests."

Her nostrils flared. "What about my self-respect?"

"What about pleasure?" he countered in low, rippling tones.

She responded with another shiver.

He pressed his advantage. "Why do you continue to deny that you are a sensual creature? Pleasure itself is not wrong, nor is it wrong to want it."

"It is outside of marriage." She wrapped her arms around herself.

"And is marriage any guarantee? Did your husband know how to satisfy you, Kit? When he rose from your bed, did he leave you still aching for his touch?"

"Stop it," she moaned.

"Did he worship your body with his? Treat you as a cherished lover?"

"Stop! Please." She closed her eyes, and her breath came in shallow gasps.

He edged toward her. "I am merely trying to open your eyes to the possibilities that life has to offer."

Her eyes flew open. "Possibilities? How can you say that when physical gratification is all you want?"

He allowed himself a sardonic smile. "What else is there?"

"Your view of the world is rather limited, my lord. What about love? Or has such a concept never entered the scope of your philosophy?"

He raised an eyebrow at her. "I fail to see why we need to complicate things unnecessarily."

"Then you have never been in love?"

"I never said that." He shifted uncomfortably in his top boots. "But love tends to make matters worse between a man and a woman. People who fall in love almost invariably end up hating one another. Why bring such emotional rubbish into what is otherwise an amicable arrangement?"

"Have your mistresses never fallen in love with you?"

"Some have."

"Then they must be the owners of the broken hearts Her Grace mentioned."

"Perhaps, but most of them knew better, as I hope you

will. Kit, what I'm offering is not wicked or immoral, and not as prison-like as marriage."

"Not immoral?" she echoed, clearly outraged. "How can you say that? You flit from one woman to the next without care or cause!"

"Most married women do the same thing. As long as they are discreet, their *affaires* are their own business."

"Just because most married women do it doesn't make it right. In all the years I was married, I never even considered such a thing."

"Never?" He quirked a sardonic brow.

A bright flush stained her cheeks. "Never."

"But would you have, if the right opportunity had presented itself?"

"No!"

"But you are no longer married, are you? You're free to make your own happiness, and I'm offering you just that—the chance to enjoy yourself with no unreasonable expectations attached. You will still have your freedom, Kit; I would never infringe upon that. We shall go to the opera, the theater, Vauxhall Gardens. Attend poetry readings and philosophical discussions. We could even travel back to India, if you wished. I would make you happy, Kit, more than you have ever been before."

He could read the indecision in her face.

"If you think Her Grace is right," he murmured, "and that life is an adventure, then what are you so afraid of? We need each other, Kit, whether you know it or not."

She hesitated, holding her breath for a moment. Then she exhaled with a soft sigh. "All right," she breathed. "I accept. But we must first negotiate the compromise between the duke and the dowager. I will not . . . I will not become your mistress until that part of the bargain is complete."

"That is fair," he replied. His smile turned suggestive. "Now, how shall we seal our agreement?"

She hesitated, then held out her hand.

The marquess took it, turned it over, and placed a gentle, feathery kiss on her exposed wrist. She gasped and snatched back her hand.

"Remember," he said, "no more running away. Know what you want, and do not be afraid to pursue it."

She glared at him. "You are the very devil, my lord."

He chuckled. "I know."

He let her go then, and she hurried past him down the hall, half walking, half running. He watched her, admiring the sway of her hips beneath the fabric of her dress, until she disappeared around the corner. Not once did she look back at him.

Who was this woman? Wexcombe held her in utter contempt. His great-aunt thought her nothing less than a saint. What was the truth? He had less than a week to find out and form his own judgment of her character. She had passed his first test. Now he would have to see how well she followed through.

Guilt nagged at him. He'd put her in an untenable position. If she proved not to be an adventuress, then he'd owe her one hell of an apology. If she was, and this bargain scared her off, then the dowager duchess was probably better off without her.

He supposed he could have done worse. A man of lesser morals would have seduced her outright, or made this bargain with her fully intending that she become his mistress. Unfortunately, he was not such a man. Wexcombe seemed to think he was, and there was no point in trying to convince him otherwise. His cousin rarely changed his mind once he'd formed an opinion, and he would never admit to being wrong. In that, he was as inflexible and unyielding as the dowager. Stubbornness was definitely hereditary.

He found himself wondering how she lived, what her life was like. All he knew at the moment was that she dressed like a drab little mouse, and that although she spoke with great passion about poetry and philosophy and India, she had no friends save the dowager. Her life seemed to revolve solely around the elderly woman, and that did not bode well.

If Mrs. Mallory was serious about this compromise and actively helped him to achieve it, then he would not, of course, expect her to fulfill her portion of this agreement. But he would still have to live up to his reputation and make the pretense of seduction until she proved herself as good as her word. A passionate woman lay buried beneath that severe hairstyle and those dowdy gowns; her response to his kiss had told him that. He just hoped he could keep his head on straight while playing this gambit through to the end. If not . . . there was more at risk here than the dowager duchess's happiness. But it was only a week. Surely he could behave himself for that long. Couldn't he?

What had she done?

As she hurried back to her room Kit's slippered toe caught on the Persian carpet, and she stumbled a bit. She righted herself, mentally cursed herself for her clumsiness, and continued on at a more sedate pace, though her heart continued at a gallop within her chest. Her skin tingled as though she had stood too close to a fire, and a deep, aching warmth pooled low in her belly. She cursed herself again, this time for responding to the marquess's sensual persuasions.

Lunacy. Sheer and utter lunacy. That scoundrel had her cornered, and he knew it.

When he had started to speak to her about the dowager duchess, he had sounded so kind, so concerned. Her lips twisted in a sneer. An act, every word of it. He cared for no one but himself. Oh, he might regard Her Grace in a fond, patronizing sort of way, the way one might a favorite pet, but when it came down to issues of her welfare, he was content to let others take the responsibility.

To think she had turned to him for help. Foolish, naive girl! Trusting an opportunist was like trusting a cobra; it sat coiled, appearing inert, then would lash out without warning. And she'd certainly been bitten.

But they had made a bargain, and he was bound by honor to help her. She wouldn't think too closely about what she would have to do when the matter was finished. A shudder racked her. His comment that he would respect her freedom—gammon. What did he know about her freedom? He had never spent hours alone with only books for company, never been told to marry someone he hardly knew not only because the family needed the money but because he would likely never receive another offer. He never had to endure seven years of marriage to someone twice his age with little tact and less wit.

Kit slammed her chamber door behind her, then leaned her back against it. Always duty and honor. Duty, and honor, and obligation. She squeezed her eyes shut against the tears that even now gilded her lashes. She would do her duty to the duchess—she had to. She had always done what was expected of her, first to her family and later to her husband.

Yes, she would honor her bargain with this handsome, heartless devil. But for once in her life she wanted to follow the demands of her own heart.

Chapter Five

*L*ate the following morning, after another nearly sleepless night, Kit went down to breakfast. A quick survey of the breakfast room revealed the duke seated at the head of the table, his head barely visible above the edge of the newspaper. No one else. Kit realized she'd been holding her breath, and exhaled in a slow sigh. The sound attracted the duke's attention; he peered over his newspaper, scowled as he recognized her, then snapped the paper back into place. Knowing from yesterday's experience that trying to speak to His Grace alone was fruitless, and not overly fond of the idea of trying to eat beneath the duke's scathing glare, Kit wrapped a scone in a napkin and retreated to the terrace.

Morning sun bathed the formal garden in a glow of gentle light. Blooms burst forth in a profusion of color, especially in the well-tended beds of roses for which Broadwell Manor was famous. Lavender scented the air; heavy-headed irises nodded in the slight breeze. The laburnums wore long trusses of yellow flowers. A few insects buzzed through the warm, humid air. A flash of color behind a boxwood topiary caught her eye, and Kit headed toward it.

She passed along a series of gravel paths that radiated outward from the middle in a maze-like lattice. At the center of the garden stood a fountain, a structure that involved two winged cherubs pouring water from pitchers into a single immense basin. Water splashed and gurgled in counterpoint to the ringing birdsong.

The dowager sat on one of the stone benches that ringed the basin, her shoulders hunched beneath her fringed shawl. In her dress of grass green silk, with a wispy lace cap perched atop her gray curls, the elderly lady reminded Kit of a dandelion that had gone to seed. Her face looked pale and drawn despite the spots of rouge on her cheeks.

Kit put two and two together: the duke's surly mood and the dowager's depression. A yawning pit opened at the bottom of her stomach. Not already! She sent a fervent prayer heavenward. *Oh, please, not the children. Don't let him have threatened to keep them away from her....*

The dowager did not seem to hear the crunch of gravel beneath the heels of Kit's half boots, but continued to stare into the empty basin of the fountain. Kit worried her lower lip between her teeth, then pasted a bright smile on her face. "Good morning, Your Grace," she called. "How lucky we are to have such fine weather."

The dowager glanced up then, and her unhappiness vanished beneath an answering smile. She straightened. "Good morning, child. Yes, fine weather indeed. Come and sit with me."

Kit sat obediently, then began to unwrap the scone. "You seemed rather melancholy just now, Your Grace."

"Did I? Well, I shall have to stop that at once. How can I be melancholy when you are here?" she said, a twinkle in her dark eyes.

Kit placed a gentle hand on the lady's arm. "Are you feeling well, Your Grace?"

"Of course I am well, child. Never better. Why do you ask?"

"I heard that you had quarreled with the duke," Kit replied as delicately as she could, "and that you took to your bed after you returned from your outing."

"Oh, pish," snorted the dowager. "Afraid my grandson will give me apoplexy, what? You know I am not so weak and frail as all that."

"No, not at all, ma'am," Kit hastened to amend. "But I was concerned for you, especially after you took dinner in your rooms."

"You needn't be, child. I just could not stand the thought of eating while that sour-faced grandson of mine glared at me from across the table. The prospect was enough to curdle my stomach."

Kit's hand closed over her scone. "I know what you mean. I trust you are recovered this morning?"

"Quite, although I would feel a good deal better if my relations would stop meddling in my affairs," the dowager declared. "I am prodigiously displeased. I made my wishes quite clear when I told them I wanted to hear no more of their nonsense, but they have not paid any heed."

"Would you like to leave?" Kit asked quietly. "We can be back in Bath before nightfall."

"No." The dowager shook her head. "I will not turn tail and run from this bumble broth, child, and give my ninny of a grandson even the smallest sense of victory. Leaving now will only postpone the inevitable. No, we shall stay the entire week and sort out this mess once and for all. Unless, of course, *you* wish to leave."

Kit jerked up her head, startled. "Oh . . . no, Your Grace."

"I must say I am glad to hear it, my dear. We shall show them that we're made of sterner stuff, what?"

"Of course," Kit murmured. She glanced down at the napkin on her lap, the scone a rather crumbly mess in the center of it, and folded it back up and set it aside, her appetite gone. Apprehension coiled in the pit of her stomach, and remained no matter how hard she tried to dispel it. She would not be the one to suggest that they leave Broadwell Manor, even to get away from the marquess; she could not break her word, nor would she cry coward. This was about the dowager's happiness, not hers.

Lord Bainbridge's words to her yesterday in the gallery told her exactly what he wanted from her, just as his kiss had told her that he was not a man to be put off.

His kiss.

Embarrassed heat scorched her face. Why on earth had she allowed him to bait her like that? To talk of seduction—she blushed again—in such a frank and open conversation? What a great looby she had been! The marquess had planned the whole thing from start to finish; he had probably been the one to suggest to the dowager that he return to the house to "check on" her. And she had fallen neatly into his trap. But her body had betrayed her. She had luxuriated in the sensation of his lips over hers, of his strong arms enfolding her body. She twitched. No matter how much she enjoyed it, she would not let him seduce her, not until he had followed through with his part of the bargain. Her fingers tightened on the edge of the bench.

"I was right, you know," commented the dowager.

"I beg your pardon?" Kit sat up in an instant.

The elderly woman regarded her with speculation. "Woolgathering, child? That is unlike you. Is anything the matter?"

Kit's blush intensified. "No. Please go on, Your Grace."

"I was merely going to say that my suspicions are correct, that my grandson and the rest of the family are plotting against me."

"Plotting against you?" Kit repeated. She flinched. She really must stop doing that. "What makes you say that?"

"Not only did they have the gall to tell me that it is high time for me to retire to the dower house in Wiltshire," she huffed, "and to stop embarrassing them with my exploits and odd starts, but this morning my grandson actually threatened to keep the children away from me unless I accede to his wishes. Of all the cheek!"

The pit in the bottom of Kit's stomach yawned wider. Oh, God, it was as she feared. They would have to act quickly, before a compromise became impossible.

"The duke may have spoken in anger," she soothed. "After all, the two of you are quite alike in your temperaments."

"Well, I suppose so," grumped the duchess. She hesitated. "I have never embarrassed you, have I child?"

"No, Your Grace," Kit insisted. She reached out and gave the dowager's hand a reassuring squeeze. "Never. And you know I am truthful enough to tell you what is *de trop*."

"Dear child"—her eyes grew moist, and she cleared her throat—"I do not know what I will do if I cannot see my great-grandchildren. Perhaps . . . perhaps it is time for me to retire."

"Do not give up hope, Your Grace." Kit's mouth hardened. "The week is not over. Something may yet be done to make the duke see reason."

"Reason?" erupted the dowager. She fumbled for her

handkerchief. "That oaf will see reason when pigs grow wings."

"The duke is uncommonly stubborn," Kit admitted. "Then again, Your Grace, so are you."

"I?" The dowager drew herself up.

Kit shrugged. "You are, ma'am, and you know it."

"Oh, well, I suppose I am. But not as stubborn as he is."

Kit struggled to hide her grin; such a gesture would only goad the duchess to further heights of indignation.

Then the duchess looked toward the house. "Ah, here comes my great-nephew—we shall ask his opinion. Good morning, Bainbridge."

Kit froze.

The marquess strode down the center path with a jaunty gait, one hand raised in greeting. He cut a handsome figure this morning in his jacket of charcoal gray superfine, buff inexpressibles, and highly polished Hessians. Kit forced her gaze to focus at the level of his snowy cravat, no higher; to look into his eyes meant ruin.

"Good morning, Your Grace. Good morning, Mrs. Mallory," he called as he drew close.

"Good morning," Kit muttered between clenched teeth. She had been relieved to avoid him at the breakfast table, and yet here he was. And, from the teasing light in his dark eyes, she could see he was quite pleased with himself for having found her.

Bainbridge made an elegant leg. "You are looking well, Mrs. Mallory," he said. "I am delighted to see that your megrim no longer troubles you."

The nerve of the man! Kit glared at him. "Thank you, my lord, but I fear another pain has come along to take its place."

He grinned.

The dowager looked askance at her. Kit raised her chin.

"I have brought some good news," he announced. "If the weather cooperates, we shall picnic on the lakeshore this afternoon."

"A picnic?" The dowager raised a doubtful eyebrow. "And whose suggestion was this?"

He cocked his head toward her. "Her Grace thought it might give us all a chance to enjoy each other's company in a more informal setting, and to allow the children to spend some time with you."

Kit threw a wary glance at the marquess. A picnic? The fussy, prim-and-proper duchess had proposed a picnic? Her eyes narrowed. Fustian. Either this was Lord Bainbridge's doing, or the duke was putting the screws to his grandmother, showing her just what she would be denied if she did not capitulate. How could anyone be so cruel? She pressed her lips together.

A visible struggle between delight and despair crossed the dowager's face. "Well, I must compliment my granddaughter-in-law on such a fine idea. The children will be delighted."

"Take heart, Your Grace," Kit said softly. "Everything will work out."

"Has something happened?" the marquess asked, frowning.

The young woman regarded him sadly. "His Grace has issued an ultimatum. If the dowager does not do what he says, he will prevent her from seeing his children."

Bainbridge swore under his breath. Then he straightened his shoulders, reached down for the dowager's hand, and bowed over it. "I assure you, ma'am, that I will not allow this to happen." He shot an intent look at Kit.

A sad smile curved the dowager's lips. "You are a dear

boy, Bainbridge, but I doubt you will be able to change that ninny's mind. He can be so damnably stubborn."

"He can indeed, ma'am," agreed the marquess in a steely tone. "But so can I. Mrs. Mallory and I believe we might be able to make him rescind his decision about the children."

"Oh you can, can you?" The dowager looked pointedly between the two of them. "And what hugger-mugger is this?"

Bainbridge lanced another significant glance at Kit. "Mrs. Mallory and I spoke yesterday afternoon regarding our mutual concern for Your Grace's happiness, and we may have come up with a plan."

An odd expression crossed the dowager's face. "And what sort of plan is this?"

"Both you and the duke are very set on having your own way," Kit ventured.

"Are you calling me bullheaded, child?" demanded the dowager.

Kit did not flinch. "Yes, Your Grace. Both of you are stubborn, bullheaded, and obstinate. If both of you insist on getting your own way, then both of you will end up monstrously unhappy. Lord Bainbridge and I care for you a great deal, and neither of us wants to see that happen."

The dowager's eyes narrowed. "What are you getting at, child?"

"Very well, ma'am—I shall be blunt. We want to find a compromise, something that will satisfy both you and the duke."

"A compromise?" The dowager's painted brows shot upward.

"Yes, Your Grace."

Just as quickly, her eyebrows plummeted into a scowl.

"Well, if by compromise you mean giving in to that little twit, I won't do it."

"But, Your Grace—"

"I won't do it. I will not let that young popinjay dictate to me. I will not!"

"Please, Aunt," Bainbridge began.

The dowager rose, her bosom puffed out like a pigeon's. "I had thought better of you, Bainbridge, than to ask me to surrender my dignity. I will not budge, do you hear? Not one inch!" With that, she pulled her shawl around her and swept down the garden path.

The marquess grinned as he watched Her Grace flounce into the house. "I think that went rather well, don't you?"

Kit rolled her eyes. "Well? She categorically refused us!"

"What did you expect?"

Kit put a hand to her temple. "I don't know. Suspicion, doubt, relief . . . anything but an explosion like that. This will not be easy."

"Did you think it would be? Did you think we would propose this cozy arrangement and have everyone agree to it just like that?" He snapped his fingers.

"No, of course not," Kit snapped, irritated.

Bainbridge rubbed his chin. "We are dealing with two very proud, very obstinate individuals."

"That much is obvious, my lord," she replied with no little sarcasm.

He sighed. "I'm saying that we must proceed with caution. I fear that both of us speaking to the dowager like this put her on the defensive; she suspected that we were trying to force her to change her mind."

Kit considered a moment, then bit her lip. "I had not thought of that," she admitted. "So what do we do now?"

The marquess clasped his hands behind his back. "I propose a two-pronged attack: I will deal with the duke while you plead our case to the dowager. Then, and only then, do we put them together to finalize the agreement."

"Do you think we can succeed in only a week?"

"We must, if we don't want them to be completely forlorn for the rest of their lives. And I, for one, don't particularly like dealing with miserable people; they tend to make everyone around them miserable, as well. Short of locking them in a room together and refusing to let them out until they agree, I see no other option."

Kit picked up the linen napkin and toyed with one embroidered edge. "All right. Now that we have settled on a method, what sort of compromise do we intend to propose?"

Bainbridge began to pace on the path in front of her. "That should be simple enough."

"Then why haven't they come up with it themselves?"

"Because everyone in this family takes a sort of perverse pleasure in being difficult."

"I'd noticed," she mumbled.

He chuckled. "Let us look at the facts. Wexcombe wants his grandmother to retire to the dower house."

"Which Her Grace will not even consider," Kit said.

"So she says. And now the duke has threatened to keep her from seeing the children."

She sighed. "Which will break her heart."

"We need to come up with an arrangement that will give them both what they want."

Kit nibbled on the end of her thumb, her brows drawn in a pensive line. "What if . . ." Her voice trailed off.

"What is it?" prodded the marquess.

"What if the dowager duchess agreed to stay at the dower house for part of the year, say . . . from Lady Day to Michaelmas. The rest of the year she would be free to travel. The chill winters prove difficult for her, but she could spend that time in Bath, or even in a warmer climate if she wished. It would mean no more prolonged voyages to India, but I suspect she will be able to live with that."

Bainbridge gazed at her with dawning comprehension. "And if she is at the dower house during the Season, Wexcombe wouldn't have to worry about any of what he calls her 'embarrassing exploits.' And she can spend the summer with the children, which will delight them all to no end. It's perfect."

"I only hope Their Graces agree," she murmured.

"We shall have to ensure that they do. It is my hope that the picnic this afternoon will put everyone in an amiable frame of mind, and receptive to our suggestion."

"I will see if I can speak to the dowager before that," said Kit. She picked up her napkin and climbed to her feet. "I want to apologize for upsetting her."

"Good luck, then. And Kit?"

He'd used her nickname. How intimate it sounded coming from him! Against all reason, a tiny spark of delight shivered all the way down her spine. "Yes?"

He held out a hand to her. "Well done."

She stared at his broad, calloused palm and remembered what had happened the last time she'd given him her hand to kiss. With an insouciant smile, she dropped her napkin-wrapped scone into his grasp. "Thank you, my lord," she said, then turned and marched back to the house.

His resonant chuckle drifted after her.

That afternoon, a carnival atmosphere reigned along the shore of the lake below Broadwell Manor. A large blanket had been spread beneath one of the stately oaks that grew not far from the lake, with liveried footmen putting away the remains of the repast that only recently covered it. Woven picnic hampers large enough to hold the small feast sat off to one side. Rowboats sat snugged up to the pier; the duke, in his shirtsleeves, rowed the duchess across the middle of the lake's placid blue surface. By the water's edge, Emma and Nathaniel shouted and clapped with joy as the dowager presented them with toy wooden boats, complete with canvas sails. The nearest Kit could tell, judging by the shrieks and yells and vocalized booms, was that the dowager was playing a menacing Bonaparte, while the children and Miss Pym defended the shores of England as the Royal Navy.

Kit laughed and took one last bite of her apple, relishing the crisp burst of flavor on her tongue. Never did an apple taste so good as it did on an idyllic afternoon, and this one certainly qualified for the honor; so far, no one had spoken so much as one angry or provoking word. That was mostly due to the interference of the marquess, who managed to deftly change the subject whenever the conversation took a dangerous turn.

The marquess. Her eyes seemed to stray to him no matter where he was, and at the moment, he and Lady Elizabeth were walking along the shore of the lake, engrossed in conversation; the drifting wind carried the lady's trill of delighted laughter to Kit's hearing. Her fingers tightened on what remained of her apple, and she flung the core as far as she could.

Why would she be upset that the duchess's sister was flirting with him? Or was he flirting with her? She unclenched her fingers and flexed the tension from them. He was an unrepentant rake, after all. She should expect as much from him.

So why could she still taste bitterness at the back of her throat?

Another burst of laughter, this time of the juvenile sort, diverted her attention. The dowager climbed the gentle slope toward the trees, accompanied by the bouncing children and the red-faced and perspiring Miss Pym.

Kit waved. "Did your new ships keep England safe from that Corsican monster?"

"We blew Boney-part up!" Nathaniel exclaimed, then laughed uproariously.

"And he won't come back!" added Emma, not to be outdone.

Kit applauded. "Good show! That will teach him." She turned to the dowager. "How very obliging of you, Your Grace, to act on behalf of the enemy."

"Someone has to," the dowager chuckled. She lowered herself onto the blanket, waving away the two footmen who hurried to assist her. "Go away, you foolish boys. When I need your help, I will ask for it."

Kit hid her grin behind her hand. She cleared her throat. "So what will you do now that England's greatest enemy is vanquished?"

"We came back up here because the children have asked for a story," said the dowager. She slanted Kit a look rife with mischief. "But I have told them that your stories are better than mine."

"*My* stories?" Kit echoed.

"Yay! A story! A story!" yelled Emma.

"Lady Emma, control yourself!" huffed Miss Pym, an expression of abject horror on her round face.

The dowager frowned and waved a dismissive hand in the governess's direction. "Oh, enough of your harping, woman. Let the children be children, for heaven's sake!"

Miss Pym fell silent, abashed.

"Now then," continued the dowager, "I have told Emma and Nathaniel that you have a favorite story about a prince who goes on a quest to find his princess. You should know it by heart; you've been working on it long enough."

"Indeed I have," Kit agreed with a laugh.

"Please, Kit?" Emma pleaded.

"Please?" echoed her brother.

Kit raised her hands. "All right. I will tell you the story."

Emma and Nathaniel appeared ready to erupt in yells of triumph once again, but a quelling look from Miss Pym nipped any such impulses in the bud. Still wriggling with excitement, the children began to settle on the blanket.

"What is all this commotion about?"

Kit's heart leaped into her throat at the sound of the marquess's voice—whether from pleasure or annoyance, she couldn't tell, but she didn't want to think about it too closely.

"I . . . I was about to tell the children a story, my lord," she faltered. She raised a self-conscious hand to the battered chip-straw bonnet she wore as the marquess and Lady Elizabeth drew near. In her gown of lemon yellow sarcenet, with matching ribbons and plumes on her bonnet, the earl's daughter appeared more prepared for a fashionable tea party than an informal picnic.

"A story!" cooed Lady Elizabeth. Her pale blue gaze spat poison. "How delightful. I'm sure you're simply wonderful at telling stories."

"Indeed," Bainbridge seconded. A faint smile quirked his lips. "May we join you?"

"Well, I don't know . . . ," Kit said, tapping one finger against her cheek.

"Oh, come now," the marquess drawled. He winked at her.

She replied with a raised eyebrow. "Very well, my lord, but I will require that everyone participate."

"What's party-see-pate?" queried Nathaniel, his face scrunched in confusion.

Kit smiled down at him. "It means that everyone gets to act out a part of the story."

"That sounds fun!" Emma proclaimed. "May I be the princess?"

"Of course you may," Kit replied. "Nathaniel, would you like to be the prince?"

Nathaniel's enthusiastic nod was quickly overridden by his sister.

"Why can't Lord Bainbridge be the prince?" demanded Emma, with a shy glance at the marquess.

"Because I have other plans for him," Kit said blithely. "Now, the title of this story is the *Ramayana*, which means 'The Story of Rama.'"

Emma piped up, "Who's Rama?"

"Shhhhh, child—don't interrupt," advised the dowager. Emma bit her lip and fell silent.

"Rama was a great prince," Kit began, warming to her role as storyteller. "He lived in a great city called Ayodhya, and he was a very good and wise man, and a skilled soldier."

Nathaniel popped to his feet, grinning.

Kit paused a moment. The *Ramayana* was an epic; telling the entire story would last well into the night, not to mention bore the children to tears, so she decided to stick with the most interesting portions.

"Emma, you will be Princess Sita, Rama's beautiful wife," she continued. "And Your Grace, I would be most pleased if you would play the part of Hanuman, a great monkey warrior."

"A monkey?" blurted Lady Elizabeth. "How rude!"

"Not at all," chortled the dowager. "You see, Hanuman is the embodiment of cleverness and devotion. Very good, child, very good. I shall do my best."

"What about me?" drawled the marquess, a teasing slant to his mouth.

"You, my lord," Kit replied with asperity, "will be Ravana, the ten-headed demon king."

"A demon? Interesting." His smile broadened. "I've been called worse."

"I assume you have a part for me," said Lady Elizabeth.

"There are not many women in the *Ramayana*, so I will have to think a bit. . . . What about Trijata?"

Lady Elizabeth raised a perfectly arched brow. "And who is Trijata?"

Kit made a moue of embarrassment. "She is a *rakshasi*—a demoness."

"Well!" huffed Lady Elizabeth, her lips compressed.

"Well, of all the *rakshasi*, she is one of the kindest," Kit added, torn between mortification and laughter. "She consoles Sita after Ravana has kidnapped her and imprisoned her in his garden."

"This is all in fun, Lady Elizabeth," purred the marquess. "Surely you can play along."

"Oh, very well." But she did not look pleased.

With everyone eager to play their designated roles, Kit began the story. She started with Ravana's abduction of Sita from the forest and her imprisonment in Ravana's garden in the island kingdom of Lanka. Emma played a tearful Sita to the hilt, rubbing her eyes and pretending to cry.

Kit went on to tell how Prince Rama sent Hanuman to find Sita and give her Rama's ring as a token of his love and devotion. The dowager, her face alight with merriment, pretended to dodge imaginary demon hordes until she reached Emma's side. Then the two of them sat down at the edge of the blanket, giggling.

Finally, Kit staged a rousing battle between her diminutive Prince Rama and the much larger Ravana; Nathaniel took on the marquess with glee, wielding a stick sword, until Lord Bainbridge gave a mighty groan and fell to the grass. Ravana's "death" was greeted with cheers and enthusiastic applause. The marquess climbed to his feet and bowed.

"It didn't hurt when I cut off your heads, did it?" Nathaniel asked.

"Not at all." Bainbridge winked at him. The boy grinned.

Kit's heart turned over. He was so at ease with the children; it was not hard to imagine him with a little boy and girl of his own. Dark-haired children with green eyes . . . She bit her lip and chided herself for being so foolish.

She praised each of her players, and made sure everyone, especially the children, received a round of applause. After a curtsy to her audience, Emma beamed, then gave a huge yawn.

With that, Miss Pym apologized, saying it was past time for the children's naps. She gathered the protesting Nathaniel and Emma, then started back toward the house. The marquess stretched himself out on the blanket, his laced fingers pillowed under his head, his eyes closed. Lady Elizabeth asked him if he would row her across the lake; he declined. When he also declined to show her the folly, called the Temple of Virtues, Lady Elizabeth declared that she had had too much sun and would retire to the house. She flounced back up the hill.

"Well, that's much better," announced the dowager. "I was beginning to think we'd never have a moment's peace."

Kit chuckled, then became aware that the marquess was watching her through slitted lids. She gave him a warning glance, then pointed with her chin down to the lake. He smiled lazily and closed his eyes. Kit pursed her lips. What was the matter with him? If he would but leave, she could negotiate with the dowager. But he showed no inclination to move, drat him.

After a few moments, the dowager levered herself to her feet. "I do believe I will go down to the temple and see what my grandson is up to," she announced.

"Let me help you," Kit volunteered, and started to get up.

"No, no, child. Stay where you are. You look comfortable, and I fancy a bit of a walk. I shan't be long." Humming to herself, the elderly woman started back down the hill.

Kit cast a glance over her shoulder—and then looked with more alarm. The footmen had disappeared. She was alone with the marquess. The back of her neck grew warm.

"I really should go with the dowager," she said, rising to her knees.

Bainbridge put a hand on her arm. "No more running away," he murmured.

"I am not running."

A laugh rumbled from his chest. "No, you were going to walk at a very hurried, yet still ladylike pace."

"What do you mean by this?" she demanded.

"By what?"

"The footmen have very conveniently gone missing," she said with a hiss of indrawn breath.

"What if they have?"

"Did you dismiss them?"

"Yes," he admitted with a shrug. "I wanted to spend some time with you without the presence of overly curious eyes and ears."

"Why?"

He gazed at her with a thoughtful frown. "You seem to labor the impression that no one wants to spend time in your company. Do you think yourself so unworthy of attention?"

"Just of yours, my lord."

He released her arm, then cocked an eyebrow at her. "My dear Kit, perhaps I am mistaken, but somehow I get the distinct impression that you do not trust me."

"Oh, you are not mistaken in the least, my lord," she shot back.

"When I asked you yesterday, you didn't give me an answer. So I'll ask you again—what are you so afraid of? Men? Or is it just me?"

She ducked her head. "No," she mumbled.

"Well, then, sit down. You have nothing to be afraid of; we are still in full view of Their Graces, so I won't be able to ravish you. At least not now." He smiled, reached back, and opened one of the picnic hampers.

"What are you—?"

He put a finger to her lips. "I have a surprise for you."

Chapter Six

With a flourish and a wide, wicked grin, Bainbridge presented the bowl to her.

The veiled suspicion vanished from her beautiful green eyes. "Strawberries? This is the surprise?"

"Why? What were *you* thinking of?" he asked with a chuckle, and popped a small, slightly overripe fruit into his mouth. Juice stained his fingers; he licked them off, his gaze never leaving hers.

She blushed a very becoming shade of pink. "I . . . I . . . Oh, never mind."

He selected another strawberry and presented it to her. "Have one. They're very good."

The lovely widow hesitated. Her fingers twitched. Then, with thumb and forefinger carefully aligned, she plucked the fruit from his grasp and ate it.

"You see?" he murmured, and set the china dish between them. "It's exactly what it seems to be."

"And are you, my lord?" she asked.

"Am I . . . what?"

"Are you exactly what you seem to be?"

He paused with a strawberry halfway to his mouth. "Why do you ask?"

Her nostrils flared. "You have a most annoying habit, sir, of answering a question with another question."

"Do I? I hadn't noticed." He chuckled.

She took another piece of fruit from the bowl and contemplated it. "I asked because I know so little about you."

Bainbridge felt his smile dwindle. "I am a rake and a scoundrel, my dear, albeit a very well-bred one. What more do you need to know?"

She glared at her berry, then at him, as if she were considering throwing it at him. Then she sighed and ate it. "I do not know how they do things in London, sir, but if I am to be your mistress, I would like to know a bit more about you than that."

"But you will not be if our gambit is not successful. That was our bargain."

"We will succeed," she said quietly. "We must. So I believe the two of us should become better acquainted with each other."

A strange sensation began deep in his stomach. For a moment she sounded as though she had resigned herself to success . . . and to becoming his mistress. What was she up to? Was she trying to throw him off his guard, or was her curiosity as innocent as it sounded? Most women seemed content with the knowledge of his name, title, and yearly income, with a few other obscure details thrown in as window dressing, but he was quickly coming to realize that Katherine Mallory was not like most women. He lounged back onto one elbow. "What do you want to know?"

She selected another berry. "I've told you something about what my life was like when I was young. What about you?"

Damn. With one swift thrust, she'd gotten down to

things he would gladly forget, if given the chance. "My upbringing was rather ordinary," he hedged.

"What about your family? Do you have any brothers or sisters?"

"I had a brother. He died when I was ten." He bit into a large berry, and relished the sensation of his teeth ripping through the yielding fruit.

Her eyes rounded. "I'm sorry," she whispered.

The berry turned tasteless on his tongue. He gulped it down. "You're bound to hear the story eventually. Nothing titillates the *ton* so much as scandal, even twenty-year-old scandal."

"You do not have to tell me, my lord, if the memory pains you so."

"I am not such a coward as all that, ma'am," he said with a humorless smile. " 'Tis a simple tale, so I will be brief. My mother and father loved each other once, or so they claimed, but by the time I was five they hated each other with a passion. I suspect that was the one thing in their lives about which they felt anything at all. When I was ten, my mother left, and tried to make us leave with her. I refused to go, but she took Geoffrey."

"How old was he?" she asked quietly.

"Six." Bainbridge stared up into the patch of cloud-scattered sky visible through the branches of the tree. "My father rode off in pursuit, of course, but my mother, I learned later, went to great lengths to avoid him, including urging the coachman to breakneck speed. The wheels hit a hard rut in the road, the axle snapped, and the carriage crashed to flinders. My father found them moments later. No one survived."

Kit sat motionless, one hand raised to cover her mouth. Telltale moisture glistened at the corners of her eyes.

"No need to shed tears on my behalf," he said, his voice rough. "My mother never cared a whit for anyone but herself. We were well rid of her."

"I do not believe that for a moment," Kit murmured. "I'm sure she loved both you and your brother very much, and that is why she wanted to take you with her. If she hadn't loved you, she would have left you behind without a second thought."

"I suppose that is one theory." His lips curled in a sneer. "But I rather believe she wanted to torture my father by taking away his precious sons."

"You mentioned something yesterday, that people who fall in love end up hating each other in the end. This is what you meant—it happened to your parents."

"My parents were not the only ones foolish enough to make a love match. Among the members of the *ton* you see dozens of lovestruck newlyweds mooning over their spouses one year, then taken up with paramours the next. Love is a pointless complication in one's life."

"Was your father bitter?"

Bainbridge turned away, lest Kit see in his face any shadows of the memories that haunted him. He felt her light touch on his shoulder.

"It's all right," she said.

His eyes narrowed to mere slits. "I do not want your pity, madam."

"No, my lord," she countered quietly. "Not pity. I would never condescend to offer you that. Understanding and sympathy, yes, but not pity."

A few brief moments ago he had advised her to stop running away from what she feared; could he do any less? He sighed. "I can only tell you what happened before I was packed back off to school. How he locked himself away in his study for days at a time, doing nothing but drinking and staring at a miniature of my mother. The countless bottles of claret and brandy he imbibed to drown his sorrows. The opium smoke that clung to his clothes when he finally stumbled home by the early light of day. I was not particularly surprised when they told me he died of an overdose."

She gave his shoulder a gentle squeeze. "Oh, Lord Bainbridge . . . ."

"Nicholas," he said roughly. "My name is Nicholas. I have just revealed to you one of my most dark and painful secrets, so I suppose you are entitled to my name, as well."

He heard her exhale with a slow, deliberate breath. "Is your parents' tragedy the reason why you have never married, Nicholas?"

He clenched his teeth. "Perhaps it is. I shall have to marry eventually, but when I do I shall ensure that my impeccably pedigreed bride holds not one ounce of affection for me."

"But—"

The marquess shrugged off her hand. "Enough, Kit. I do not wish to say anything more about my past, checkered as it is."

She withdrew her hand and rubbed at the palm. "All right."

He rolled onto his side to face her. "Now it is your turn."

"Mine?" Her gaze shuttered.

Bainbridge picked up a strawberry and rolled it between his fingers. They were like two duelists, exchanging shots with words instead of bullets. He had just withstood her barrage, and now he was not about to delope. "You told me you wished to become better acquainted, Kit. Soon we shall have no secrets between us—physically, at least. I have just answered your question; now you can answer one of mine."

She paled, then raised her determined chin. "Very well."

"Were you happy in your marriage?" His gaze fixed to hers, he ate his berry in one bite.

She managed to turn paler still, her deep golden freckles standing out in stark contrast to her ashen complexion. "My lord, I do not—"

"Nicholas," he amended. "You started this, my dear. No running away, remember?" He offered her another ruby red fruit.

This time she was not so careful in taking his offering; her fingers grazed his. Heat flooded through him right down to his toes. Lord, if he wasn't careful, he'd end up with *two* mistresses.

"Were you happy?" he prodded.

"I was comfortable." She looked away.

"That doesn't answer my question. Comfort does not equal happiness."

She ate her berry, then made a face. "I thought I was happy, at first. I was living in this beautiful, exotic place, far away from my avaricious father, and for the first time in my life I never had to worry about money."

"What made you change your mind?"

Kit sighed. "I soon realized that I had traded one selfish man for another. My father cared for nothing but money, and my husband cared for nothing but his collection."

"Collection?" Bainbridge frowned. "What sort of collection?"

"Over the years George had accumulated all sorts of trophies: tiger skins, elephant tusks, and the like. He delighted in them for a while, but over time he lost interest and went in pursuit of the next item. Soon after we reached India I realized that I was but another of his trophies—the aristocratic wife he'd brought back from England to grace his home." Her mouth twisted. "Or I should say, rather, the wife he'd bought in England. He'd given my father a handsome settlement in exchange for my hand."

Bainbridge muttered an oath under his breath.

She hadn't heard him; her eyes had glazed over. "He made a great fuss over me in the beginning, buying me silk saris, jewels, all sorts of trinkets. But after about three months, when the novelty had worn off, he went in search of other conquests and left me at home to wonder where he'd gotten himself off to this time."

"You must have been very lonely," Bainbridge said softly.

"Not at first. I was too busy adjusting to this new life of mine. I'd gone from being a rather sheltered young girl to the wife of a prominent merchant, in a place that teemed with color and noise and stench. George would go off on tiger hunts and other such excursions, which would take him away for weeks at a time. I used that time to explore my surroundings and to learn more about this strange new world.

"Of course, when George discovered I'd been acting with what he called too much independence for a simpleminded female, he quickly curtailed my activities 'for my own good,' as he put it. I was not on a Grand Tour, he told me, but his wife, and I should begin to act like it." She laughed, a high, brittle sound. "Thankfully, he was never at home for long."

"Is that why you never had children?"

He expected her to take umbrage at that highly impertinent question, but instead she blushed, and a fresh barrage of tears threatened her composure. He offered her his handkerchief, but she waved it away.

"I miscarried a child about a year into our marriage," she whispered. "There, Nicholas. There is my dark and painful secret. George said it was probably for the best, but that I would have to try harder next time. The next morning he went off on another hunt."

"That bastard," Bainbridge growled through his clenched teeth.

With a listless hand she picked up another berry, then returned it to the bowl. "Looking back, I suppose I should have been relieved."

This time it was his turn. "I'm sorry," he said. "That must have caused you a great deal of pain."

She nodded. "Yes . . . So much that I thought I would run mad. Once I recovered, I found I desperately needed a diversion, something to occupy my mind. Since I shared very few interests with the other English ladies in Calcutta, I had to look elsewhere. Then one morning I heard my maid, Lakshmi, talking to her husband in their native tongue, and I decided I wanted to learn. We had so many Hindu servants, and I thought it could only be beneficial that I learn to speak their language.

"George never knew what I was doing; as long as I kept house for him and presided over his endless balls and dinner parties, that kept him happy. Over the next several years I learned to read Hindi as well as speak it; then I discovered the *Ramayana*, written by the poet Tulsīdās in the sixteenth century. I'd seen parts of it performed in puppet plays, and that made me want to read the entire epic. Once I had read it, I was determined to translate it into English, and that has sustained me until now."

"Is that what the dowager meant when she said you had been working on it long enough?"

She nodded. "Books were my most constant companions as a child; in India, they were my salvation."

"Salvation through literature," Bainbridge mused. "I know a few Oxford dons who would go into spasms of rapture at the very concept."

She ducked her head, her face hidden by the brim of her drab bonnet. "I have relied upon my books ever since. You will think me craven for it, but I do not know how else I would have survived."

He shook his head. "I do not think you craven, but you must know when to set your shield aside."

"I beg your pardon?"

"You cannot hide behind your books forever, Kit. Is that your idea of freedom?"

She blinked. "Well, no . . . I suppose not. But I haven't been hiding."

"Have you not?" he countered. "Going around in those dowdy gowns, not wanting anyone to notice you?"

Her eyes sparked with anger. "W-what? How dare you!"

"I dare, my dear, because I should hate to see such loveliness and spirit go to waste. What do you want from your life?"

She laughed, but there was no mirth in it. "The dowager has asked me the very same thing."

"And?"

Kit glared at him, then took a strawberry from the bowl and bit into it. "What does it matter to you, my lord? Once our bargain is complete, you shall have what you want."

"But after you and I part company, Kit—what then?

Will you go back to your cave and cover yourself once more in sackcloth and ashes?"

"Enough!" she cried. "Why do you insist on provoking me?"

"Why do you insist on denying yourself any true contentment?"

"I *am* content. And you're doing it again, my lord."

"Nicholas," he reminded her with a grin.

"Nicholas," she agreed with impatience. "Now please stop asking me these insufferable questions. You are not entitled to know what is in my heart."

"I think I already know," he murmured. He ignored her startled expression, and continued. "You've been hurt, Kit, hurt and disappointed by the very men who were supposed to protect and care for you. Now that you are on your own, you have chosen to insulate yourself behind a wall of books and call it freedom."

She paled. "No," she whispered.

"Then what would you call it?"

"I . . . I don't know." She seized her lower lip between her teeth.

He leaned in closer to her. "Kit, all your life you have run away from the things that made you unhappy. No more of that, remember? It's time you faced your fears."

"Stop trying to tell me how to live my life," she snapped.

He shrugged. "Then stop hiding and live it."

Her mouth opened, closed, and opened again, like that of a fish caught out of water. He stared at those berry-stained lips, lush and red and ripe, and another wave of awareness swept through him. The breeze blew tawny wisps of her hair onto her forehead; he resisted the urge to reach out and brush them back. A hint of her perfume grazed his senses. Lord, how had he let this woman affect

him so? He had not thought that the strange paradox of
worldliness and sheltered inexperience would make for
such a powerful aphrodisiac.

"Do you want that last strawberry?" he asked, all innocence.

She flicked a glance down at the bowl. "No, you may
have it."

He gave her his most charming smile. "Would you
hand it to me? Please?"

Kit hesitated, then held it out to him. He gently
grasped her wrist, then leaned down and enveloped the
berry, and her fingertips, with his lips. His tongue
brushed warm and wet against her fingers, licking the
juice from them before she yelped and yanked away her
hand.

He savored the fruit, its flavor mingled with the taste
of her skin. "Think about what you want," he repeated,
his voice low and intent. "And if that happens to be me,
then I will be happy to oblige you."

Kit gaped, then pulled away and struggled to her feet.
She looked down at him, her face filled with indignation.
"If you put as much energy into convincing the duke as
you do into seducing me, my lord, then we are certain to
meet with success. At this moment, however, I cannot
help but wonder where your priorities lie."

He relaxed back onto his elbows. "I shall keep my part
of the bargain," he assured her.

"See that you do." She turned and gathered her skirts.
"Now if you will excuse me, I must return to the house."

"All right, Kit. I will let you go, for now. But remember . . . you cannot run away forever."

She straightened, glared at him, then marched up the
hill without so much as a backward glance.

The marquess stared after her; a thoughtful frown

pulled at his brow. Wexcombe was wrong about this woman; he was sure of that now. No one could pretend the pain he had seen on her face just moments before. She was no adventuress, nor did she have any designs on the dowager's fortune. She did not even know what she wanted from herself.

So now what was he going to do? He didn't know how long he could keep this up; it would take all his self-control to sustain this pretense and still keep his hands off her. God, the more he touched her, the more of her he wanted. He should stop this charade right now and tell her the truth—any honorable man would—

No.

He grimaced. If he told her why he'd really proposed this bargain, that the whole thing had been a test, a ruse, how she would react? Well, at this point he could make a fairly good guess: she would be furious to find out what he'd done—lied to her, manipulated her, trifled with her, and generally acted like a complete cad, good intentions be damned. And after what she had revealed to him, his conscience would not let him sleep at night knowing he'd just added to her list of betrayals and disappointments.

His conscience? Hell, a rake wasn't supposed to have a conscience. What was the matter with him?

Bainbridge groaned and flopped onto his back. This situation had become much more complicated than he'd intended. He'd gotten himself into this mess, and he would have to get himself out. The sooner he convinced the duke to compromise about his grandmother, the sooner this would all be over. He would just tell Kit that she'd convinced him of the value of her freedom, and that they should go their separate ways, with no regrets or obligation. Or would she take that as yet another rejection, and retreat further into her shell?

And why did he care so much for what happened to her?

Bloody hell!

He shoved a hand through his hair. He would become a monk. Yes, that was it. As soon as this was over, he would take holy orders, seal himself up in a spartan cell in a monastery somewhere, and never so much as look at another woman again. Never mind that he would likely go mad within a month; it would prevent him from getting himself into any more of these damnable scrapes.

In the meantime, he'd better be on his best behavior—even if it meant putting an end to the seductive teasing that came so naturally to him. He would just have to be careful around her. Very, very careful. Of course, as with all his good intentions, he would have to see just how long it lasted.

Kit sat at her dressing table, staring at her reflection in the mirror. She didn't *look* any different. But as for how she felt, she might as well be another person entirely.

She gazed down at her fingertips, rubbed them against her lips. The touch of Lord Bainbridge's—Nicholas's—mouth on her skin had made her whole body thrum with awareness, and with—yes, she would admit it—desire.

He wanted her. She had no idea why, but at this point it hardly mattered. He wanted *her*. Katherine Mallory. Widow, wren, and aspiring ascetic. She pulled a face. Put that way, she did not sound appealing in the least.

She stared harder at the looking glass. Unappealing, and yet Nicholas saw something in her that attracted him, something hidden beneath this wretchedly practical hairstyle and the tentlike gowns she'd grown accustomed to wearing. He wanted her, and made her *feel* wanted. Desired. Attractive in a way she'd never felt before.

Kit put a hand up to the thick, tight chignon coiled at the back of her head and slowly pulled out the pins that kept it restrained, until her tawny golden hair, like a lion's mane, came tumbling around her shoulders and down her back. She picked up a comb from the dressing table and began to run it through the heavy waves. But after the comb caught for the third time, she tossed it aside with a growl of frustration.

George had loved her hair; he had called it her crowning glory. Actually, the way he had said it made it sound as if her hair were her only glory. She lifted a heavy lock, twirled it between her fingers, then returned her gaze to the mirror.

Her own anguished green eyes regarded her from the glass. All this hair, so heavy and long and unmanageable, with not even so much as a few kissing curls at the temples to soften the strong line of her jaw, seemed to suffocate her. She was drowning, drowning in a mass of long, unfashionable hair, and in oversized drab gowns that didn't become her in the least—which, now that she thought about it, was why she had chosen them.

It couldn't be wrong to want to be pretty, could it? To be as pretty and desirable as Nicholas made her feel? The dowd in the mirror was not her. Not really. Neither was she the gaudily dressed parrot she had been when George was alive. Who was she, then?

The marquess had asked her what she wanted from her life. The dowager had told her that she must seize happiness for herself. Was a life alone, surrounded by her books, all she had to look forward to? Was that all she wanted? Her lips firmed.

Logic dictated that if she wanted to be happy, she had

to do something about it. Nothing would happen if she sat here moping in front of her looking glass.

Kit clenched her hand around the lock she held and sighed. She would start here. George had loved her hair. All the more reason to cut it.

She summoned her maid.

"Lakshmi," she said, her eyes never leaving her reflection, "I want you to send for Epping, the dowager duchess's abigail. Ask her to come and cut my hair."

The sari-clad woman's dark eyes reflected the sheer horror on her face. "But, *Memsahib!*" she protested in melodically accented English. "All your beautiful long hair. . . . Surely you cannot mean to do such a terrible thing!"

Kit flashed a nervous smile. In India, women did not cut their hair save as a sign of deepest mourning for a husband. "This has nothing to do with George's death, Lakshmi, nor does it reflect on your skills as my maid. I am tired of all this weight hanging from my head. Epping does Her Grace's hair, and she will know what is fashionable. Please ask her to come here at once. Quickly, before I am tempted to change my mind."

Lakshmi pressed her palms together in a reverent *namaskar*, then departed, but Kit thought she heard the woman muttering in Hindi about "mad Englishwomen."

First the hair, then . . . Kit fingered the plain material of her skirt and made a moue. A pity she could not do something immediately about the state of her wardrobe, but she would make it a priority when she returned to Bath. After all, Nicholas wouldn't want her to dress like a drab little wren when she was his—

She swallowed around the sudden lump at the back of her throat, then forced herself to acknowledge the word.

His mistress.

A shiver coursed through her slender frame. Nicholas's mistress. Every proper instinct in her body rebelled at the concept, but another part of her, a part of her she had not known existed before now, fairly quivered with excitement. To be desired by such a devilishly handsome man without the constraints of marriage. . . . The idea gave her a wicked thrill.

But what about love?

Kit lowered her head, her hair forming a veil around her face. Yes, there would be a part of her that would want to be cherished and loved, but that was more than what Nicholas had to offer. Would being with him, and being desired by him, be enough?

It would have to be. For the dowager's sake, she had made a bargain with the devil himself, and after today she was certain he wanted to collect. Duty and honor demanded that she follow through.

Still, one question nagged at her: how on earth would she be able to surrender only her body to Lord Bainbridge without risking her heart, as well?

Chapter Seven

*W*hen Kit entered the yellow drawing room, she discovered that she was the last to arrive for dinner. The moment she stepped across the threshold, five pairs of eyes pinned her where she stood. Once again, everyone was staring at her. At least this time she knew why.

She dipped a brief curtsy. "Good evening."

"Why, Mrs. Mallory, I do believe you have done something different with your hair this evening," said the duchess, her cool blue gaze roaming over Kit with thinly disguised antipathy.

Kit started to raise a self-conscious hand to her head, stopped herself, then laced her fingers together so they would stay still. "Indeed, Your Grace," she replied. "With the weather growing so warm, I thought a shorter style would be more comfortable. I wonder that I didn't think of it sooner."

"So do we all," muttered Lady Elizabeth, her hands contracting like claws around the arms of her chair.

The dowager peered at Kit through her lorgnette. "It becomes you, child, I must say. And not before time."

The duke said nothing, but he shot a significant glance at Lord Bainbridge, who stood by the sideboard.

The marquess ignored him. "Indeed. Most fetching." He gestured to a half-full decanter on the sideboard's polished mahogany surface. "May I offer you some ratafia before dinner, Mrs. Mallory?"

"Yes, thank you, my lord," Kit replied, in danger of having her breath leave her body altogether. His dark, velvety gaze hardly left her for a moment, even when he poured the liquid into a glass for her.

"Charming," he murmured as he handed it to her. "You are full of surprises today, Kit."

Her fingers brushed his; a slight flush rose to her cheeks. The way he was looking at her was enough to turn her limbs to jelly. Good heavens, if she had known that a simple change of hairstyle would affect such a change in her appearance, she would have done it long ago.

Epping, the dowager's abigail, had worked wonders with her heavy mane. She had not allowed Kit to look in the mirror while she snipped ever closer to the young woman's neck. Instead, Kit had focused, with increasing trepidation, on the growing pile of tawny locks accumulating on the carpet around her chair. But the results were worth every moment of doubt.

Free from their bonds, her newly shorn locks had sprung into attractive waves that took a curl with ease. Under Lakshmi's scrutiny, Epping then pinned most of the curls up into a loose knot at the crown of Kit's head, but left a soft collection to frame her face. This new coiffure emphasized the graceful line of her neck and the slightly tip-tilted set of her eyes. While hardly a bird of paradise, at least she no longer looked like a drab little wren. And from the way the marquess was staring at her, like a hungry man outside a sweetshop window, she could tell that she was not the only one pleased by her alteration in style.

"And I must say your timing is impeccable, Mrs. Mallory," commented the duchess.

Kit took a sip of her ratafia and tried to appear unaffected by Her Grace's cutting tone. "And why is that, ma'am?"

"Oh, did I not mention it to you? A few days ago His Grace and I received an invitation from our neighbors, Lord and Lady Sherbourne, for a ball at Shering Park tomorrow evening. Everyone is welcome, of course."

"How . . . ah . . . delightful," Kit managed to reply. The ratafia had turned to dishwater on her tongue. Tomorrow evening? She knew full well why the duchess had not said anything to her, but it hardly mattered. She had not been to a society party in eight years, and never hoped to go to one again, truth be told. Her heart slid upward into the back of her throat at the very thought.

The duchess must have seen Kit's hesitance; a satisfied smile curved the lady's thin lips. "We will understand if you choose not to attend, considering the recent death of your husband."

"What poppycock," blustered the dowager. "Of course she will go. 'Tis high time she was out in society again. Do you not agree, child?"

Kit did, indeed. The marquess had been right all along; it was time for her to stop running. Ignoring the fluttering sensation below her breastbone, she raised her head. "If Your Grace wishes it."

"Well, I do wish it," blustered the dowager. "What say you to that?"

"Then I would be pleased to accompany you," Kit declared.

"Good." The dowager sat back in her chair with a gusty sigh. "Then it's settled."

"I do hope you will save a dance for me," Lord Bainbridge said softly.

"Only one, my lord?" she teased, and the marquess rewarded her with another of the slow, seductive smiles that set her blood on fire.

The butler then arrived, and announced that dinner was served. The duke offered his arm to his grandmother and the marquess escorted the duchess, leaving Kit and Lady Elizabeth to walk behind.

"A pity about the Sherbournes' ball," commented Lady Elizabeth, her tone sugary sweet, her gaze poisonous. "You won't have time to acquire a new dress to match your new coiffure. I would loan you one, of course, but I fear it would be much too small."

Kit's smile grew frost at the edges. "Thank you for the offer, Lady Elizabeth, but I shall manage."

Lady Elizabeth stared suspiciously at her, as if wondering what sort of barb lay beneath the cordial words, but Kit paid little attention to her and went in to dinner. It would take more than a spiteful cat like Lady Elizabeth Peverell to overset her any more than today's events already had.

After supper, the family returned to the drawing room to play cards. Instead of seeking her out, as he had before, the marquess sat down with the duke, duchess, and Lady Elizabeth for a hand or two of whist. Kit stood in the doorway, torn between disappointment and relief. Gracious, whatever was the matter with her? One moment she was swooning over the marquess like a starry-eyed chit just out of the schoolroom, the next she felt like a fox cornered by a particularly determined hound. Before the end of the week she would have to decide which role she wanted; there would be no turning back.

"Come and play piquet with me, my dear," called the dowager.

The elderly lady regarded her with unabashed curiosity, and the tips of Kit's ears grew warm. She crossed to the dowager's table and lowered herself into the lyre-backed chair opposite Her Grace.

The elderly lady shuffled the cards. "You look lovely tonight, child."

Kit responded with a slight smile. "Thank you, Your Grace. I hope you do not think me too impertinent to make free with Epping's services, but you had not yet returned to the house, and I knew I had to send for her before I lost my nerve."

The dowager chuckled. "In this case, I do not mind at all. In fact, I am pleased to see you've come to your senses," she declared, and began to deal.

"Come to my senses?" Oh, Lud. Not again. Had they been in private, Kit would have smacked her forehead with the heel of her palm. If she parroted one more phrase this week, she would lose patience with herself completely.

"Yes. That is, I am assuming this change in style means you have decided not to become a nun, after all." The dowager slid a sly glance at Kit from behind her cards.

"No, indeed, Your Grace. I have concluded that the life of an ascetic would not agree with me." Kit's gaze strayed over to the marquess before she forced it back to her cards.

"Well, I could have told you that," chuckled the dowager. "Now look to your discard, child."

Kit surveyed her hand, but her mind was not on the

game. She glanced again at the marquess. No, not on the game at all. She decided to change the subject; with any luck, she could distract the dowager as well as herself.

"Did you enjoy the picnic this afternoon, Your Grace?" she asked, sorting through her cards.

The dowager beamed. "Oh, indeed I did. Emma and Nathaniel are an absolute delight. A bit rambunctious, but that is to be expected at their age. Every time I see them, they have grown so much that I vow I hardly recognize them." A hint of sadness colored her words.

"Do you not see them very often?"

Her Grace shook her head, the lappets of her lace cap swaying. "Not as often as I would like."

"There is a remedy for that situation," Kit offered. "If Your Grace will consider it."

The dowager's dark eyes narrowed. "What are you getting at, child? I recognize that look on your face, like butter wouldn't melt in your mouth. You are up to something."

"You asked me to Broadwell Manor to help you, Your Grace, and that is exactly what I am attempting to do."

"Yes, but I did not ask you to side with my jailers." She set her discard down with a snap, her mouth compressed in a narrow line.

"Your Grace," Kit chided, "you know me better than that."

The dowager frowned at her cards. "Well, then, what would you call it?"

"I care very much for your happiness, ma'am, just as you care for mine. And the last thing I want is to see you shut up in some cold stone box of a house for the rest of your life," Kit insisted. "You would do no better there than I would in a nunnery."

One of the dowager's artificially darkened brows

twitched a bit. "I cannot deny you that point, child. Go on."

"Lord Bainbridge and I believe we may have found a solution that will allow you to retain much of your independence, placate the duke, and let you see your great-grandchildren in the process." Kit gazed at the elderly woman over the edge of her cards. "Would you like to hear it?"

"I am listening."

Kit lowered her voice. "The compromise would work thus: from Lady Day to Michaelmas you reside at the dower house in Wiltshire. That way you will be able to see the children whenever you please, and especially when they are home from school for the summer."

"And the rest of the year?" queried the duchess archly.

"The rest of the year you would be free to travel. To take the waters at Bath, or seek a warmer climate entirely, and escape England's beastly winters."

"I see." The dowager tapped one finger on the table. "But I need not remind you that six months is not nearly long enough to travel to certain places and back again."

Kit raised an eyebrow. "Oh, come now, ma'am. On the *Daphne* I recall you saying very clearly how much India, and especially Indian cuisine, disagreed with you."

"Hmph." The elderly woman made a great show of sorting her cards. "And you and Lord Bainbridge hatched this scheme together, did you?"

"As you are well aware, Your Grace."

"What does my grandson have to say about this?"

Kit glanced over at the marquess from beneath her lashes. "I do not know, ma'am. Lord Bainbridge volunteered to propose the matter to him, but I cannot say whether or not he has had the opportunity to do so.

Please, Your Grace, I ask you to at least consider our proposal."

"Oh, very well. I shall consider it," huffed the dowager.

Kit's eyes widened, and her heart gave an excited little leap.

"But," the elderly woman added, "I will not agree to anything unless my grandson apologizes for his reprehensible behavior of late. He has no respect for his elders. To think he would hound and badger me—his own grandmother!—in such an appalling manner. The very idea!"

Kit sighed. Never had she dealt with two such difficult and willful people. "Then at the same time, Your Grace, you should consider apologizing to him for calling him a popinjay, a ninny, and an arrogant pup."

The dowager regarded her first with outrage, then with a touch of embarrassment. "Hmm. Well, I suppose you have a point, child."

"Yes, I do, ma'am," Kit maintained. If the dowager duchess was going to be difficult about this, then by Jove, so was she! "Both of you are equally to blame for inflaming the situation, and it is past time for you to set the situation to rights. No, do not bother to argue with me, Your Grace. If this is the only solution that will provide you a measure of satisfaction, then I will not allow you to throw it away for the sake of your dratted pride." She sat up in her chair, back ramrod straight, lips pinched.

The dowager raised her lorgnette and stared through it. "My goodness, child. I had not thought you capable of such fervor."

"I am resolute, Your Grace. More than I have ever been in my life."

The elderly woman set down her glasses. "So I see.

Very well, my dear. I may be a trifle bullheaded, but I am not a complete fool. If my grandson will go along with this arrangement, then I shall agree to it, as well."

Kit let loose a sigh of relief. "Then I shall speak to Lord Bainbridge, and he will take up the issue with the duke. It is my fervent hope that we can settle this matter by the end of the week, before we return to Bath."

"Are you looking forward to it?" asked the dowager. "Returning to Bath, that is. I realize that this week has not been the most enjoyable of holidays, but somehow you do not seem at all anxious to leave."

Kit fixed her attention on her cards. "What makes you say that, Your Grace?"

"You and my great-nephew appear to have become quite cozy over the past few days," the dowager commented. Although her tone remained light and conversational, Kit knew better.

"Out of necessity, Your Grace, I assure you," she replied with a noncommittal shrug.

"Is that all?" The dowager lifted an artificially darkened brow.

Kit could not contain the sudden flush that spread over her neck and into her cheeks. "We share a concern for your happiness, ma'am, but nothing more than that."

"Hmm." The elderly woman paused a moment, and appeared to concentrate on her cards. "Pity."

Kit frowned. "I beg your pardon?"

The dowager waved her hand in dismissal. "Oh, never mind me, child. I am merely mumbling to myself. Let us continue with our game."

During the course of the evening, Kit found herself getting soundly trounced, which prompted Her Grace to make a few acerbic comments on Kit's lack of attention. But she could not help herself. Her wandering thoughts focused not on the cards, but on the dowager's perplexing comments.

Unthinking, she played the queen of hearts, only to have the dowager follow suit with the king and take the trick with a crow of triumph.

Kit ventured another glance at the marquess. Was she in danger of losing her own heart? She had asked her reflection that same question a few hours ago, and she was no closer to the truth now than she was then. Logic dictated that such a notion was pure rubbish. After all, how could she love a man she had not known any longer than a week, a man she barely knew? A man who did not condemn her for her background or her connections? A man who made her feel as she never had before? A man who was handsome, amiable, compassionate, intelligent, daring, and very, very wicked?

A man with whom she had bargained to become his mistress?

Kit did not wish to think about such questions too closely, for she feared she already knew the answer.

Yes, she was in very great danger. Very great danger, indeed.

Late the next morning, Lord Bainbridge reined his gray gelding, Achilles, to a halt a short distance behind the Temple of Virtues. His lips quirked. To think that he had asked Kit to meet him here, of all places, when virtue was the farthest thing from his mind. But the house had too many curious ears, the largest of which belonged to Lady Elizabeth.

Not that he had anything against the duchess's sister, mind you. She was quite appealing—if one happened to like clinging vines. Lud, the little vixen had all but thrown herself at him and professed her undying love when he had emerged from the duke's study this morning. He had eventually pried himself away from her, but Tolliver, his valet, had been most distressed by the sad creasing the young lady had given his lapels. Surely his light flirtations over the years had not given her any ideas; at twenty-two, Lady Elizabeth should know better. She'd had four Seasons, and turned down offers from any number of bucks more handsome and well heeled than he. He shrugged. Yes, he would have to marry eventually, but when he did he would not choose a woman who would choke the life out of him with her constant need for attention. He wanted someone who would not see him as merely a title, a yearly income, or a trophy. Someone who could see beyond his reputation to who he really was. Someone like Kit.

He blinked. Good God, where had that come from?

He slid from the saddle with unusual awkwardness and landed with a thump on the springy turf. Achilles turned his great head and whickered. The marquess gave the gray's neck an absent pat. "I'm all right, old fellow. I just find myself easily distracted these days."

He let the reins dangle, and Achilles immediately put his head down to graze. Bainbridge rubbed the back of his neck, perplexed by this strange notion. Marriage? To Kit? What had put that into his head? He did not have time for such flights of fancy; he had business to attend to.

He found Kit pacing inside the folly's domed rotunda, her hands clasped behind her back, staring fixedly at the inlaid patterns in the marble floor. Sunlight filtered through the stained-glass panels in the arched ceiling, creating a halo over her gold-crowned head. She had done her hair up again today, and he found his gaze drawn to the soft, diminutive curls at the nape of her neck. For a moment, a brief moment, he wanted nothing more than to run his lips over those downy swirls and feel her shiver with pleasure. Then he shook himself. Damn it, he promised himself that he would be more guarded, and these indulgent fantasies were anything but.

Fortunately, she had not heard him approach, and so did not notice him staring. He sent silent thanks heavenward, then leaned against one of the stone urns inside the entrance to the folly and forcefully cleared his throat.

Kit jumped. "Nicholas! You startled me."

God, how he liked the sound of his name on her lips. Those lush lips that all but begged to be kissed . . . Ah, no more of that, if he valued his sanity.

"Forgive me for interrupting you," he managed to say. "If you prefer, I can come back another time. . . ."

"Stop teasing." Her face seemed to glow with anticipation as she hurried toward him. "What did the duke have to say?"

"What, not so much as a 'good afternoon'?" He grinned at her. "You wound me, madam."

She scowled back at him. "You are a wretch, my lord, and you delight in tormenting me."

"Only because I love to watch your eyes shoot those delightful green sparks."

"What nonsense," she blustered, but he could see a rosy pink flush steal across the high-arched planes of her cheekbones. She retreated a pace. "Please tell me what happened. Did you meet with the duke?"

Bainbridge held up his hands and relented. "All right—I shan't tease you any longer. Yes, I met with His Grace about an hour ago. Wexcombe was not exactly overjoyed at the idea of a compromise, but I think I managed to make him see the wisdom of it."

"And how did you do that?" she asked, skeptical.

"At first I pointed out that this arrangement would keep both of them content, but he was still determined to have his own way. Then I simply stated that I did not agree with his assessment of the dowager's limitations, that I did not appreciate his high-handed manner in dealing with her, and neither would the *ton* once I let slip what he had done to his own grandmother."

"Never say you resorted to such underhanded methods." The hint of a smile hovered at the corners of her mouth.

He shrugged. "I did. Wexcombe does not care a fig for what Society thinks of him—he is a duke, after all—but he will go to great lengths to avoid any hint of scandal. He is rather proud."

"So I had noticed," she replied with a trace of annoyance. "How should we proceed from here?"

"Wexcombe has planned a meeting with his bailiff this afternoon, and with the ball at Shering Park this evening, perhaps we had best wait until tomorrow morning. Everyone should be in an amiable mood, and we can settle this issue once and for all. And then . . ."

"And then—what?" Her gaze slid away from his face. The tip of her pink tongue darted out to moisten her lips.

Bainbridge's mouth went dry.

Tell her the truth, you great oaf. Tell her and regain your sanity!

"Do not tell me, Kit, that you still cringe at the thought of being my mistress," he heard himself say. "Is the prospect so unpleasant?" So much for honesty.

Her incredible jade eyes widened. "N-no," she stammered. "Not unpleasant. Merely . . . unnerving."

"How so?"

"As I told you yesterday, my lord, I hardly know you."

"Oh, please, my dear Kit, not another of your virginal protests," drawled the marquess. "I thought we were past those."

"Hardly, sir," she reproached him. "I told you I have every intention of fulfilling my portion of our bargain. Indeed, I am resigned to it."

"Resigned?" He raised an eyebrow. "How lowering. You do my reputation as a rake no credit, sweet Katherine."

"I should hope not, my lord. But I am curious. . . . Any number of London beauties must be eager for your company. Is that not so?"

"True," he admitted. His brow inched upward another notch. What was she getting at?

"Then why me?"

"I beg your pardon?"

"I am no Toast, sir, nor a diamond of the first water. My looks are too . . . unusual to conform to the standard of English beauty celebrated by society. So what is it about me that prompted you to propose this arrangement, rather than simply agreeing to assist me?"

Tell her.

What could he tell her? *My deepest apologies, Mrs. Mallory, but I only pretended to seduce you in order to discover the true nature of your character?* God, that disgusted even him, the rake who had never claimed to possess an ounce of principle when it came to the fairer sex. Until now. But he had not pretended his attraction to her, which even now was enough to drive him mad.

Kit waited, gazing at him expectantly.

"You seem to labor under the misconception that you are undesirable," he replied, choosing his words with care. "But I fail to see why."

Her gaze did not waver. "That does not answer my

question, my lord. Is it simply because I am a widow, and therefore fair game?"

"No, although it does add spice to the equation."

"Ah." Disappointment clouded her eyes.

"And as for your perceived lack of beauty, Kit, I disagree with you. True, you will never be an English rose, but I think of you more like some exotic flower transplanted from a faraway garden."

She started. "I was not fishing for compliments, my lord, I assure you," she said with an embarrassed laugh.

Bainbridge grinned. "I am not offering you Spanish coin, Kit. I happen to find the combination of beauty and a strong will infinitely appealing."

Her laughter faded. "You do?"

The scent of her perfume drifted past, tantalizing him. He closed the distance between them.

"Let me show you," he breathed. He tilted her chin up, then leaned down and kissed her.

Everything about her aroused him—the scent of her skin, the soft curls that framed her face, the taste of her lips, the slender span of her waist beneath his hands. God, he didn't want to kiss her so much as devour her. Her mouth parted beneath his assault; her arms wrapped around him, and her body relaxed into his embrace. Every curve and swell seemed to fit so perfectly against him.

She tipped her head back; his lips strayed down her neck until he found the soft hollow at the base of her throat, where her pulse throbbed at a wild, almost frantic tempo. He cupped her breast, and a ragged moan escaped her.

The sound brought Bainbridge back to his senses, however temporarily. Like a man in a dream, he drew back and looked down at her. Kit remained motionless in his arms, her eyes closed, her cheeks flushed, her lips swollen from his kisses, her breath coming in shallow gasps. She was his for the taking. Dear God. If he didn't stop himself now, he'd have her propped up against one of the stone urns, her skirts rucked up about her thighs. The very thought sent another dangerous jolt of desire through him. With deliberate care, he released her. She wobbled a bit, then opened her eyes and stared at him.

"Now—never again doubt that I desire you," he said, his voice rough.

"Nicholas, I—"

Achilles's nervous whinny distracted them. Kit sprang back, a guilty look on her face, as a harried footman came pelting across the folly's stone portico.

"Lord Bainbridge?" The man halted in the doorway, gasping for air. "My lord?"

With a frown, the marquess stepped forward. "Yes, what is it, man?"

"His Grace begs you . . . to come . . . to the house . . . at once," the footman panted.

"What is it?" Kit asked, her eyes huge. "What is wrong?"

"The dowager duchess," gulped the footman. "She has taken a terrible fall down the stairs."

Chapter Eight

$\mathcal{A}$ dark pit seemed to open beneath Kit's feet. Her pulse hammered in her chest. The clammy sheen of perspiration dewed her upper lip. "W-what?"

"You must come at once," wheezed the footman.

"Has Wexcombe sent for a physician?" the marquess asked.

"Yes, my lord," the servant gasped. "But she's in a bad way."

Lord Bainbridge muttered an oath beneath his breath, then turned to Kit. "We must get back to the house—"

Kit did not wait for him to finish; she gathered up her skirts and dashed from the folly. Behind her, she heard the marquess bellow to the footman to return his horse to the stables, followed by the sound of his booted strides behind her. Together they raced up the hill and through the French doors at the back of the house.

Kit hurried toward the broad expanse of the marble staircase and started up the stairs two at a time. A small object on the landing drew her attention. She bent down to retrieve it, her hands shaking. The dowager's lace cap. With a cry, she launched herself up the stairs.

In the hall outside the dowager's bedchamber, chaos

reigned. The duchess directed an army of servants, their faces creased with worry and anxiety, in and out of the room, carrying pillows, blankets, and trays laden with cloths and basins of water. Lady Elizabeth sat crumpled in a chair in the hallway, weeping, while the duke stood over her with his fists planted on his hips, his face contorted in a snarl.

"I didn't mean to do it!" wailed Lady Elizabeth. Hysteria tinged her voice. "It was an accident, I swear!"

"An accident?" the duke roared. "You have a screaming match with my grandmother, then she just happens to fall down the stairs? Do you take me for a fool, Elizabeth?"

Kit stood in the middle of the hall, paralyzed by what she had just heard. She clasped the dowager's cap to her breast.

Lord Bainbridge pulled up by her side. "What the devil is going on here?"

Lady Elizabeth looked up at him with reddened eyes; tears streamed in long trails down her pallid cheeks. She vaulted from the chair and flung herself against him, clutching at his lapels.

"You must believe me, my lord!" she begged. "It was all an accident!"

The marquess disengaged the young woman's hands from his jacket. His dark eyes narrowed, and something in his expression—something intent and utterly ruthless—made Kit shiver.

"I think you had best tell me what happened," he snapped.

Lady Elizabeth turned pleading eyes to him. "After . . . after we spoke this morning, she accosted me and began to upbraid me in the most appalling manner. She would not stop, my lord, despite all my protests. She even followed me up the stairs, calling me the most vicious names imaginable—"

"I find that rather difficult to believe," Bainbridge interjected, the hint of a growl rumbling through his words. "What did she really say to you? The truth, Elizabeth. Now."

Lady Elizabeth paled. "She demanded that I stop throwing myself at you, and then . . . then she called me a brazen hussy who was no better than she should be!"

The marquess did not so much as blink. "And then what did you do?"

"When I reached the top of the stairs, I turned and screamed at her to leave me alone, but she was right behind me, and I think . . . I think I must have startled her, for she stumbled backward. You must believe me—I didn't mean for her to fall!"

"Good God . . . what have you done?" Kit whispered, horrified.

Lady Elizabeth shot a fulminating glare in Kit's direction, then turned in desperation back to the marquess. "I have not done anything. It was an accident. You do believe me, don't you?"

Bainbridge's mouth hardened. "Did anyone else see it happen?"

"N-no, but—"

"Then I have only your word on the matter."

"But, Nicholas, you must believe me. You love me—"

A muscle twitched at the corner of the marquess's jaw. "I thought you had more sense than that, madam. I see now that I was mistaken."

The woman paled even further.

The cold, sick feeling in the pit of Kit's stomach expanded upward until it seemed to penetrate her very heart. Nicholas and Lady Elizabeth? She shuddered, then shoved the thought from her mind. "I must see Her Grace; I cannot wait any longer."

Turning her back on the others in the hall, she rushed into the elderly woman's bedchamber. What she saw stopped her dead in the middle of the room. Tears pricked her eyes; a lump welled up in her throat. Lord, the dowager looked so still and ashen in that great bed. Her eyes were closed, her breathing shallow. Kit clapped a hand over her mouth to muffle her gasp of horror.

By the dowager's bedside, the duchess turned, recognized her, and was instantly wary.

"Let me sit with her a while," Kit begged.

"I think it best that she be with family," the duchess replied, her mouth set in prim lines.

"Please, Your Grace—just until the physician arrives."

Angry words resounded from the corridor, punctuated by Lady Elizabeth's sobs.

The duchess glanced toward the doorway and hesitated.

"Please," Kit repeated. "She is dearer to me than anyone else in the world."

The duchess hesitated. Another burst of hysterical sobbing from the hallway made her cringe. "Oh . . . very well. I must see to my sister." She departed in a swish of taffeta and closed the door behind her. Instantly, the voices in the hall dwindled to muted murmurs.

Kit drew a chair to the dowager's bedside and took the lady's hand in hers. Oh, God—her skin felt cool and clammy, and how starkly her veins stood out beneath her wrinkled skin. Ugly bruises marred her jaw and temple. She looked so very frail lying there, dwarfed by the mountain of pillows on which she rested. Tears began to overflow Kit's lashes; she wiped them away with impatient fingers. She must be strong, for the dowager's sake.

Her lower lip trembled. "Please wake up, Your Grace," she murmured. The elderly woman did not move. Another tear slipped down Kit's cheek. "I could not bear it if . . . Oh, God . . . Please do not leave me."

The noises from the hallway ceased, though Kit barely noticed. Her anxious, watery gaze remained focused on the dowager duchess, on the slight rise and fall of the lady's chest, and on her colorless, wizened visage.

She did not know how long she had been sitting there when the door opened again. She heard the shuffle of footsteps across the Aubusson carpet; then a strong pair of hands gently grasped her shoulders.

"Kit, the physician is here," Bainbridge murmured in her ear. "Let him see to Aunt Josephine. Come away."

She shook her head. "No. I want to stay with her."

"Just for a while, Kit. I promise. Come away with me."

The marquess pulled her up from her chair; her limbs felt as weak and wobbly as a foal's. With a last glance over her shoulder at the dowager, Kit allowed him to lead her from the room. Behind them, a middle-aged, portly man, his wig and spectacles askew, scurried into the room, the duke following in his wake.

Bainbridge put a supporting arm around Kit's waist and led her downstairs to the drawing room; she did not protest when he settled her on the camel-back sofa by the hearth, or when he pressed a glass into her hand. She stared numbly down at the amber liquid in the cut-crystal tumbler, then took a sip. Cognac seared a fiery trail down her throat. She coughed, spluttered, then finally swallowed. She made a face.

The marquess took the glass from her and set it aside, then sat down next to her on the sofa. "Better now?"

"A little."

"Good. Because I need to explain something to you."

"About Lady Elizabeth?" She kept her dull gaze focused on the floor.

He rubbed the back of his neck. "Well . . . yes."

"Then you need explain nothing, my lord," she replied wearily. "You are a rake. Women fall prey to your charms at the drop of a hat. I suppose I should learn to expect things like this."

"No. What happened between Lady Elizabeth and me is not what you think."

"It does not matter."

"It does," he snapped, then sat back and took a deep breath. He shoved a hand through his hair. "Please let me explain."

She gave a listless shrug. "As you wish. I do not have the energy to stop you."

"All right, then." He shifted on the sofa and turned to face her. "When Lady Elizabeth made her debut, Wexcombe asked me to dance with her; he is my cousin, and I never thought to refuse."

"You flirted with her," Kit said flatly.

The marquess spread his hands. "She was a young girl just out of the schoolroom, full of nervous jitters. I tried to put her more at ease. But I never thought about the potential consequences until today. Lady Elizabeth took those attentions seriously. She has had four Seasons, and turned down quite a number of offers. I now know the reason: she fancies herself in love with me."

Kit's heart knifed sideways in her chest. "I see."

"No, you do not. Just because she imagines herself in love with me does not mean I return her feelings."

"Of course," Kit replied with a humorless smile. "Love is an unnecessary complication, is it not?"

Swift relief crossed his face. "Exactly. I am glad that you understand."

"I do not understand everything, my lord," she countered. "Such as what prompted the dowager to confront Lady Elizabeth in the first place."

Bainbridge's gaze slid to the fireplace. His mouth tensed. "This morning, after I spoke with the duke, Lady Elizabeth accosted me in the hallway. She threw her arms around me and said she had waited in silence long enough, that she loved me and wanted to be my wife."

"Foolish girl," Kit murmured. His explanation had done little to assuage the strange, hollow ache beneath her breastbone. In fact, the more he told her, the more the pain increased.

"I told her that was impossible, of course, but she refused to listen. Burst into tears and had a grand fit of hysterics. I fear that Her Grace must have witnessed the debacle and followed Elizabeth when she fled."

"The dowager duchess can be a trifle overbearing at times, but why would she have taken such offense over what should have been a private matter between you and Lady Elizabeth?"

"I do not know," Bainbridge confessed. "Ordinarily she does not take it upon herself to chase overly forward females away from me. Whatever her reason, we shall not learn the truth of it until she awakens."

"If she awakens," Kit murmured. Her thoughts returned to the frail figure in the bed upstairs. "How could Lady Elizabeth have done such a thing?"

"I do not know. The girl can be vicious when provoked, but this . . ." Bainbridge shook his head. "Wexcombe sent her back to her parents in disgrace. She will never again be welcome in his home."

"At the moment, my lord, that is little cause for sympathy," Kit said between clenched teeth. "She goes home to her parents, while the duchess might not recover. . . ."

She bit her lip, fighting against the fresh battery of tears that began to spill over her lashes.

Bainbridge reached into his jacket and handed her his kerchief. "Here—dry your eyes. The dowager will be all right."

"How can you be so certain?"

"Dr. Knowles is the duke's own physician; I've never known a better or more competent man. Take heart, dearest Kit. Aunt Josephine has a very hard head."

Kit took the handkerchief and pressed it to her eyes. "You do not understand. She looks so pale and still. Just like my mother, right before she . . . she . . ." A soft sob erupted from deep within her.

"Shhh. It will be all right, Kitten," Bainbridge murmured, and pulled her against him. "Aunt Josephine will recover. She will be right as rain in a few days."

Kit curled against the warm, muscled strength of his chest. "I pray you are right. I could not bear to lose her."

"You will not. None of us will."

His arms tightened around her, enfolded her. She pressed her face into his cravat, inhaled deeply of his masculine scent. The steady beat of his heart resonated beneath her ear. She felt safe. Secure.

Loved.

She squeezed her eyes shut against another round of tears. He did not love her; he had all but declared himself unwilling, or even incapable, of loving a woman. This feeling might be only an illusion, but there was no harm in enjoying it while it lasted, was there?

Bainbridge gazed down at the golden head nestled on his chest, felt Kit's slender shoulders shake as he held her. There was nothing lustful or even passionate about this embrace, and yet he found it oddly appealing. Women's tears had never affected him; then again, he had most often been treated to the crocodile variety. Angelique in particular had tried to use this method on numerous occasions, and it had only served to cause him great irritation. But Kit . . . Her grief was genuine, and it moved him as nothing else had.

The marquess brushed his lips over her thick, disarrayed golden curls. Why could he not remember the last time he had comforted a woman like this? Held her, stroked her hair, allowed her to wilt his cravat with a flood of tears? A smile tugged at one corner of his mouth, then faded as quickly as it had come.

He couldn't remember the last time, because he had never done it before. In fact, he could recall several instances when he'd dismissed a woman's anguish out of hand . . . including that of his own mother. She had pleaded with him to accompany her, and all he'd done was stand there like a statue, numb with anger and disbelief, indifferent to her tears. She had been distraught about leaving, truly distraught, and he had turned his back on her. The thought appalled him.

Bainbridge gave himself a mental shake. He'd done more introspection in the past week than he had in the past thirty years, all due to the woman he now held in his arms. She needed him, and he rather *liked* being needed. Lucifer's beard. Was she a witch? Had she cast some sort of spell on him? That must be the case, for these tender feelings unnerved him more than he wanted to admit.

The mantel clock ticked away the minutes, and the afternoon sun slanted ever lower in the sky, but Kit showed no sign of wanting to move. Her sobs had dwindled, and now she lay curled against his chest, one hand still grasping the handkerchief he had given her, her breathing rough and uneven. Finally, she looked up at him, her eyes red from weeping.

"Thank you," she whispered.

Bainbridge flashed his best cocksure grin. "My dear madam, 'twould have been ungallant of me to turn away a lady in distress. The rather sad state of my cravat will bring the wrath of my valet down upon my head, but I'd say it was well worth the risk."

She attempted a smile as she plucked at the now-limp folds of his neckcloth. "You are quite the gentleman when you want to be, Nicholas."

The way she said his name made his heart constrict with longing. He brushed a stray lock of tawny hair from her cheek. "Kit, I . . ."

Heavy footsteps rang out from the vestibule. Movement caught Bainbridge's attention, and he turned his head as the duke marched into the room. His arms went slack; Kit pushed herself upright, her face suffused with a familiar rosy glow.

The duke stared at them for a moment, his eyes like chips of ice. "She's awake," he said flatly. "Awake, and asking for you, Mrs. Mallory."

Kit spared Bainbridge an apologetic glance. "I must go to her."

"Go, then," he advised gently. "And keep the handkerchief, just in case you have further need of it."

The cambric square clutched in one hand, Kit bobbed a shallow curtsy to the duke, then dashed from the room. Bainbridge watched her depart, then with a sigh slumped against the padded back of the sofa.

"Quite a cozy picture," sneered the duke. "I would never have thought it of you."

"She was overwrought, Wexcombe," Bainbridge replied, a thread of irritation running through his voice. "What else was I supposed to do?"

"Are you mad?" his cousin hissed at him. "This chit has you all but wrapped around her little finger."

"I fail to see why that has you so concerned."

"Concerned? You are supposed to get her away from my grandmother, not get tangled up with her in the process."

"I know what I'm doing," the marquess shot back.

"Do you? Another moment and you would have played right into her hands."

Bainbridge scowled. "Don't be absurd."

"No? Do you actually believe that a widow of five-and-twenty is that sheltered and innocent? That desperate for solace? Bah. You may be fooled by those immense green eyes of hers, but I know what she's about."

"And what would that be?"

The duke snorted. "Surely you have dealt with enough devious women to recognize her type. Why should she settle for the dowager's money when she can snare herself a handsome fortune and an even handsomer title to go along with it?"

"How do you think she will do that?" scoffed the marquess. "I am an unrepentant rake, remember? Wild horses could not drag me to the altar."

"It's obvious, you dolt. She's making you fall in love with her."

Bainbridge stared at his cousin as though the man had grown three heads.

Love?

He blinked. Ridiculous.

But how else would he explain it? He pinched the bridge of his nose.

Admiration—yes.

Affection, or at least a moderate amount of fondness—yes.

Lust—yes. Oh, most definitely *yes*.

But love?

Balderdash.

He sat back and waggled a finger at his cousin. "You forget, Wexcombe. I refuse to fall in love, so if that is her goal, then her plan will fall sadly flat. I prefer a much more cold-blooded approach to matrimony: find myself a chit of excellent breeding, make sure she suffers from no romantic delusions of any sort, then wed her, bed her, and get her with an heir as quickly as possible. Rather like you did, old fellow."

The duke ignored the barb. "You're getting defensive, Bainbridge, which means you know deep down that I am right."

"I do not wish to discuss it. Besides, you have no reason to worry, Cousin." Bainbridge levered himself to his feet. "She is not the schemer you think she is, nor are my actions guided solely by, shall we say, my 'baser instincts.' Now, if you will excuse me, I would like to go upstairs and check on my great-aunt."

The duke shrugged. "As you will. But never say I did not warn you."

Bainbridge strode from the room, his jaw clenched, his annoyance tempered by nagging suspicion. Had this lovely widow outmaneuvered him? His first response was an unequivocal *no*, but his cousin's words taunted him. He climbed the marble stairs slowly, as if his boots weighed as heavily upon him as his thoughts. Had Kit deliberately positioned herself as an antidote to his jaded tastes? Her modesty, her intelligence, her refreshing candor, her sheltered innocence—all of it combined into a strikingly attractive package, something he had never encountered before. Had she used his fascination to entrap him?

Perhaps. But if this was a trap, why did he not feel a greater urge to escape?

Kit rapped anxiously on the dowager's door and was ushered into the darkened bedchamber by the lady's equally anxious maid. The heavy velvet curtains remained drawn over every window, and the only light shone from a low fire on the hearth and a branch of candles by the dowager's bedside.

Dr. Knowles, who had just finished packing up his black leather bag, nodded to her as she approached.

"How is she?" Kit asked in an anxious whisper.

The portly man adjusted the wire-rimmed spectacles on his nose. "Her Grace was most fortunate. She suffered a concussive blow to the head, and her bumps and bruises are only minor. No bones were broken."

Kit exhaled slowly. Her shoulders slumped. "Thank God."

"But as I told the duke, head injuries of this nature can be tricky," he continued.

Her head snapped up. "What do you mean?"

"She may be up and about tomorrow, or it might take much longer. These things cannot be rushed. But I have every hope that, given time, Her Grace will make a full recovery. I have given her some laudanum for her pain and to help her sleep. Rest will help her heal more quickly."

"Kit?" came the dowager's querulous voice.

"Thank you, Dr. Knowles," Kit murmured.

"Of course. I shall return to look in on her tomorrow." The physician nodded to her, then took his leave.

"Kit?" called the dowager, more loudly.

She hurried to the elderly woman's bedside. "I am here, Your Grace."

A wan smile lifted the lady's lips. "Where . . . have . . . you been, child?"

Kit took the dowager's hand. "I have not been far, I assure you. How do you feel?"

"Like . . . I've . . . been sat upon . . . by . . . an elephant," the lady replied with a wheezing laugh.

An answering smile tugged at Kit's mouth. "Only an elephant? I am relieved to hear it, ma'am. We feared the worst."

"Bah." The elderly woman lifted her hand, then let it drop. " 'Twill take . . . more . . . than a tumble . . . to bring . . . me low."

"Please try to rest, Your Grace," Kit advised. "Do not overexert yourself."

The dowager frowned; her sunken eyes began to dull. "Feel . . . strange. Laudanum?" she croaked.

"Yes, the physician gave you some for the pain."

The lady blinked. "Must . . . tell . . . you," she mumbled.

Kit gave her hand a reassuring squeeze. "It's all right, Your Grace. We know what happened."

"No." The dowager struggled to raise her head, but failed. "Must . . ."

Kit restrained her. "The duke sent Lady Elizabeth away, made it clear that she is no longer welcome. She can do you no further harm."

The dowager's eyelids fluttered. ". . . would not . . . have . . . made . . . him . . . happy."

Kit leaned forward, straining to catch the whispered words. "Your Grace?"

"Had . . . everything . . . planned . . ."

Plan? What was this about? Kit shook her head; clearly, laudanum had fogged the elderly woman's wits. "Please, you must rest," she insisted.

"Dear . . . child . . ." The dowager's head lolled to one side.

As she tucked the comforter more securely around the dowager, Kit's brow puckered in a frown. What had Her Grace been so insistent about? She rubbed her temples. It didn't matter now; the dowager could tell everyone when next she awoke.

Several light taps on the chamber door distracted her. Motioning the maid to stay with the dowager duchess, Kit rose and answered the summons. Lord Bainbridge's drawn face greeted her when she opened the door.

"How is she?" he inquired in low tones.

Kit opened the door a little wider. "Dr. Knowles said she suffered a concussive injury to the head, but he believes she should recover well, given time."

"Thank God. May I see her?"

She glanced back toward the bed. "Yes, but she's sleeping. Laudanum."

"Did she say anything about what happened?"

"No," she replied, then bit her lip to prevent herself from mentioning the dowager's strange request.

The duke came up to join them, his eyes still glinting with the same cold, hard light Kit had noticed earlier. "Mrs. Mallory."

She curtsied. "Your Grace. I fear your grandmother is indisposed; Dr. Knowles administered laudanum."

His arctic gaze flicked over her shoulder to the darkened bedchamber beyond, then back to her. "That is just as well, for it is you with whom I wish to speak, Mrs. Mallory."

Kit exchanged a cautious glance with Lord Bainbridge. "I, Your Grace?"

"Wexcombe, this is really not—" the marquess began, his face taut.

The duke cut him off. "Cousin, will you be so kind as to look after my grandmother in our absence?"

Bainbridge stiffened. The two men stared at each other for a moment.

The duke cocked an eyebrow. "Surely you will not disoblige this rather modest request."

Bainbridge relented with a curt nod. A tic began in his temple. "I will stay, if you wish."

"I do." The duke motioned to Kit. "This way, Mrs. Mallory."

As Kit moved past him, the marquess seized her elbow.

"Be careful," he whispered in her ear.

Kit nodded. "I will."

"Coming, Mrs. Mallory?" inquired the duke, in a tone that brooked no opposition.

"Yes, Your Grace," she replied.

As she began to follow the duke down the hall, she shot another glance over her shoulder at Lord Bainbridge, who stared after her, a strange expression on his face. Anxiety added another loop to the knot in Kit's stomach. The tension between the two men had been all but palpable. What was going on? And after having ignored her for all this time, why did the duke suddenly wish to speak with her in private? If he was going to attempt to buy her off again, he would find her as resolute as when he made his first insulting offer.

She squared her shoulders. Whatever it was, it certainly could not be any worse than what she had already faced this week.

Chapter Nine

The duke led Kit down to the first floor, to the wood and leather-bound realm of his study. Late-afternoon sunshine streamed through the windows in a bright flood; dust motes danced in the hot, slanting beams. The stale odor of books collected but never read, mixed with the smells of fireplace ash, lemon oil, and beeswax pressed heavily against her nostrils. On the ornate stone mantelpiece a large ebony and gilt clock intoned the hour to the otherwise silent room.

"Come in, Mrs. Mallory." The duke gestured for her to precede him into the room, then closed the door behind them.

The sharp click of the latch made Kit jump. "Is this quite necessary, Your Grace?" she asked, fighting to calm her frantic heartbeat.

The duke clasped his hands behind his back as he strode across the Persian carpet. "It is. I also hope you understand that what I have to tell you must be held in the strictest confidence."

"I fail to see the need for such secrecy, sir."

He motioned to a chair. "You will. Please sit down."

Kit perched on the edge of a Chippendale chair, her

fingers laced tightly on her lap, one heel tapping a nervous rhythm on the floor.

The duke crossed to his desk, picked up a sheaf of papers, glanced through them, then set them down again. His attire—a jacket of dove gray superfine, intricate cravat, biscuit-colored breeches, and polished Hessians—exuded fashionable indolence, but the hard lines of his face and the almost military set of his shoulders, not to mention his cold, haughty gray eyes, spoiled the effect.

"I am certain you are wondering why I asked to speak to you," he began. "After all, the two of us have not been on the best of terms."

"The thought had occurred to me, Your Grace," she replied, her chin tilted in defiance.

"I assure you that I would not discomfit you thus if the matter were not of vital importance." He stood at his window for a moment, his back to her, before turning around and settling into the chair behind his desk, looking for all the world like a foreign potentate holding court. "Since you seem to favor plain speaking, Mrs. Mallory, I, too, shall be blunt. I am concerned about the growing connection between you and my cousin, the Marquess of Bainbridge."

Heat blazed across Kit's cheeks. "That is none of your business, Your Grace."

He leaned forward and rested his elbows on the mahogany desk, one cool blond brow arched at an inquiring angle. "Has he asked you to marry him?"

Kit rose slowly to her feet, breathing hard. "If you have brought me here merely to importune me with impertinent questions, then I must beg Your Grace's leave to retire."

"Sit down, Mrs. Malloy," ordered the duke in an exasperated tone. "By your reaction, I take it he has not."

Kit remained standing. "No."

"Are you certain?"

She glared at him. "If you know your cousin half as well as you claim, Your Grace, then you realize he will make no such offer."

He relaxed back into his chair. "I must say I am relieved to hear it, but not for the reason you might suspect."

Kit's brow furrowed. "What do you mean by that, Your Grace?"

"Will you sit down, or must I crane my neck to look up at you?"

Her jaw set, Kit complied.

"Better," said the duke. "Now, I must beg your indulgence, for to give you a proper explanation will take some time; I ask only that you bear with me."

"What is this all about, Your Grace?"

He steepled his fingers in front of him. "First, and I do not seek to be impertinent, Mrs. Mallory, but have you never wondered why a man like Bainbridge, a Corinthian who moves in the first circles in London, would show an interest in you, a Cit's widow?"

His patronizing tone raised the hairs on the back of Kit's neck. What the deuce was this arrogant man trying to say? She bit back a rather rude reply; she must not let the duke prick her into a display of temper. "He is a rake, my lord. Any woman can guess his intentions."

"Any woman, indeed," he murmured. "So you agree that his attentions to you seem rather . . . unusual?"

She shifted in her seat. "I do not deny that, Your Grace."

"Then allow me to enlighten you. He pays his attentions to you at my request."

Kit's mouth rounded in shock. "W-what?"

"Just as I said, Mrs. Mallory."

"But—why? You have made your disdain for me perfectly clear, Your Grace. What does Lord Bainbridge have to do with any of this?"

"When my grandmother returned from India, she could talk of nothing else but you. Even now, she spends more time with you than she does with her own great-grandchildren. I ask you—what was I to think? The dowager duchess is getting on in years, and less scrupulous individuals might seek to curry favor with her in the hope of obtaining an inheritance."

"And you thought that I—? That is despicable, sir," she hissed.

He shrugged. "I had no idea who you were, Mrs. Mallory, but I did know of your father, and his reputation was cause enough for alarm."

"And that is why you thought you could buy me off with ten thousand pounds. The apple does not fall far from the tree, is that it?"

"Ten thousand pounds would have made you quite wealthy. I could not credit the fact that you turned me down."

"I had no need of your money, Your Grace," she snapped. "Not then, and not now. Not ever."

"Yes, you are a stubborn creature. When my grandmother announced her intention to bring you here on holiday, I invited Bainbridge here to distract you."

A horrid premonition shot through Kit like a lead ball. Her eyes widened. "You asked him to . . . to seduce me?"

The duke spread his hands. "I asked him to get to know you, to charm you, to insinuate himself into your confidence."

"And then what?" she demanded.

"I wanted you away from my grandmother, Mrs. Mallory. Since you would not take my money, I asked Bainbridge to seduce you, to transfer the focus of your interest from my grandmother onto him. He intended to set you up most handsomely, then abandon you. And, after having had an illicit, very public affair with her greatnephew, my grandmother would hardly want to have any further contact with you."

Kit began to shake. "This is utterly preposterous. I don't believe you."

"You may ask him for the truth of the matter, if you wish, but I suspect you already know."

Their infamous bargain. Now she understood. It all made sense, in a strange, cruel sort of way. All the charm, all the flattering attentions. He had toyed with her, pretended to go along with her plans for compromise, all the while weaving his spell of seduction around her. The playful banter. The kiss on the hill. Their meeting in the folly. The strawberries . . .

"Why are you telling me this?" She swallowed against a sudden swell of nausea.

The duke pursed his lips. "For two reasons. First, I now perceive that I was mistaken. Your reaction to my grandmother's fall told me that you hold genuine affection for her, despite the fact that you share no blood connection. I am a proud man, Mrs. Mallory, but I know enough to admit when I am in the wrong."

Kit rose, her entire body trembling. "Do you mean to tell me that after all this, after bribing me, insulting me, and planning to ruin my life, you have had a sudden attack of conscience?"

His cold gray eyes seemed to look right through her. "Call it what you will."

"And your campaign to induce Her Grace to retire to the dower house? Was that part of your plan, as well?"

The duke did not flinch from her withering scorn. "No. But after this accident, I do not know if my grandmother will be capable of prolonged travel. The dower house may hold more appeal for her."

"I see. Very neat. And the second reason?"

"I fear my cousin still intends to follow through with his plan."

A cold void opened in the pit of her stomach. "What do you mean?"

"Even a connoisseur of beauty grows jaded over time, and seeks more . . . unusual avenues of diversion. Lord Bainbridge thinks you the antidote to his ennui, Mrs. Mallory, and will use you to amuse himself, no matter what the consequences."

"You seem very sure of this, Your Grace."

"I know my cousin."

She tasted bile at the back of her throat. "I see. Is there anything else you care to tell me?"

"Only that I owe you an apology." Placing his hands on the desk, he slowly climbed to his feet.

"An apology?" A low, hollow laugh echoed from her throat. "You astound me, Your Grace. After all you have done, I would not have thought you capable of any such thing."

"You have it nonetheless. What more do you want?"

What did she want? She wanted to wake up from this nightmare! The situation, however, called for a more practical and immediate solution. Her lips thinned. "I wish to leave Broadwell Manor. Leave, and never have the misfortune to cross paths with you again."

A strange, enigmatic smile crossed the duke's thin features. "What about my grandmother?"

"Dr. Knowles is confident of the dowager's recovery," Kit stated. "I leave knowing she is in competent hands."

"But she will be most disappointed that you did not stay."

Kit clenched her trembling hands in the folds of her skirt. "You cannot expect to abuse me so thoroughly, Your Grace, and wish me to remain under your roof. Despite any disappointment Her Grace might feel, I am certain she will understand. I shall leave a note for her that explains the circumstances behind my departure."

"There is no need," the duke said quickly, coming out from behind his desk. "I shall tell her myself, if it will spare you any pain."

Kit put the full force of her loathing behind her stare. "Do you fear any lack of discretion on my part, Your Grace, or is it that you know how your grandmother will react to your intrigues? You cannot keep the tale from her for long; she is more intelligent than you give her credit for. She will discover the truth eventually, even if I do not reveal it to her."

The duke responded with a raised eyebrow. "I thought I made it quite clear from the beginning that I expected you to hold our conversation in the strictest confidence."

She bit her lip. "So you did."

"I would never dream of insulting my grandmother's intelligence, but I also do not wish to upset her during her convalescence. I had hoped you would share that sentiment."

"Very well, Your Grace. I will not say anything to her until she has recovered. But I do intend to correspond with her while she is still here. I trust you will not interfere with the delivery of those letters."

His lips twitched. "Certainly not."

"I would like your word on the matter."

Anger flared in his eyes. "I suppose you would try to find a way around me if I did not."

"I may be only a Cit's widow, Your Grace, but I do not hold my honor as cheaply as you seem to hold yours, and I do not think you above reading your grandmother's correspondence."

"Then you have my word, madam."

"Thank you." Kit gripped the back of her chair for support as the room began to waver around her.

"My dear Mrs. Mallory, you look unwell," said the duke, suddenly solicitous. "Should I ring for tea? Or would you prefer something stronger—a glass of sherry, perhaps?"

Kit gritted her teeth. "All I require is the opportunity to depart this house with all due speed."

"You would be better advised to stay the night and start your journey in the morning."

She looked toward the window. The sun still hovered well above the horizon. "In light of all you have told me, I am resolved to leave as quickly as possible."

"Then I shall order my carriage brought around for you. That is the least I can do."

She put a hand to her throat and steadied herself. "Thank you, Your Grace—and yes, it *is* the very least you can do."

The enigmatic smile still on his face, the duke offered to escort her back upstairs. Kit recoiled away from him when he reached out his hand to her. She opened the door and all but flew up the stairs to her room. Tears blurred her vision. A heavy weight pressed against her chest, making her gasp for breath.

Dear God. What a great fool she had been. After his attempt to bribe her, she should have known the duke would try another approach. But she had never expected anything like this! She should have been more careful, more guarded. Lord Bainbridge's attentions had seemed too good to be true; she should have seen right through him. But he had trapped her as neatly as a fly in a web, and to her everlasting shame, she had welcomed it.

She paused at the top of the stairs, one hand gripping the wrought-iron railing.

If only she had listened to her instincts: Lord Bainbridge *had* been too calculated in his charm. Still she had fallen prey to it and bared some of her most intimate secrets to him in the process. Not only that, but her wanton response to his touch, his embrace, his every method of seduction, had only served to encourage him. In a few more days, she would have willingly surrendered her honor to a man who had none.

Images from the past week tormented her. The blazing kiss they had shared in the gallery. The marquess laughing with Emma and Nathaniel beneath the tree by the lake. The strawberries. God, she would never be able to eat strawberries again without remembering the silky feel of his mouth against her skin. And the tender way he had held her, comforted her after news of the dowager's injury, only hours ago. Every touch, every caress, every laugh was seared in her memory.

What a simpleton she had been!

She flung herself through her chamber door, slammed it shut, then collapsed with her back against it.

The tumult sent Lakshmi rushing out of the dressing room. She took one look at Kit's face and murmured a quick prayer in her native tongue. Then she hurried to Kit's side and gently pulled her away from the door. "*Memsahib*—oh, *Memsahib*, what has happened?"

"We are leaving, Lakshmi," Kit said flatly. "Pack our things."

"The duchess-*memsahib*—she has not? . . ." The maid's ebony eyes were saucers full of worry.

Kit shook her head. "No, she will be fine, but we cannot stay. Please, Lakshmi—no more questions. Just get us packed as quickly as possible."

"As you wish." The maid pressed her palms together, then glided to the wardrobe and began removing the clothing from its depths.

Kit, her knees still shaking, went to her writing desk and gathered her books from its surface. She glanced at the clock. As impossible as it was to believe, she had been kissing Nicholas—Lord Bainbridge—in the folly only a few hours ago. It felt like a lifetime. With a muttered oath, she set aside the books. Then she sat down, drew out a sheet of vellum, and began a note to the dowager duchess.

What would she write to Her Grace? That despite Kit's own instincts, she had fallen in love with a rake? A man who had played her like a trout on a line? Kit sighed and dipped her pen in the inkwell. No. For the moment, all she would say was that however much she regretted having to leave the dowager's side, she must return to Bath and would explain her actions later. A few days from now, when she could summon enough courage, she would relate the entire story in another letter.

Then she paused, her pen poised above the paper.

Fallen in love . . .

A large blot of ink dripped from the nib, marring the blank page. Kit stared at it. She did. She loved him. Good God. What had she done?

Kit shook herself, set down her pen, then crumpled the ruined sheet of paper and tossed it away. She pulled out a fresh page. Damn the duke for his interference. Was her life any less important because she possessed no title and no surname of dignity? And as for the marquess . . .

Angry heat crept up the back of her neck; she flexed

her fingers. Despite her shame, she refused to slink into a hole and lick her wounds like an injured animal. The marquess had taught her one thing of value: no more running. She knew what she had to do. With fresh conviction, she picked up the pen and began to write.

Kit and her maid had all but finished packing when a thunderous banging erupted from the chamber door. Lakshmi ran to open it, and Lord Bainbridge's tall form burst into the room.

"What the devil are you doing?" he demanded.

Sweet heaven—her heart turned over at the mere sight of him, and his voice sent a rush of delicious shivers down her spine. She steeled herself. "I should think that much is obvious, my lord," she replied. "I am packing."

His dark brows drew together in a forbidding line. "Why?"

"To return to Bath, of course."

"Return to? . . . I don't understand. Why this sudden departure? What about Aunt Josephine?"

Kit placed the last few items of clothing in her trunk, shut the lid, then directed the footmen to take it down to the waiting carriage. "As much as I would like to remain by the dowager's side during her recuperation, circumstances prevent my staying here any longer."

"Circumstances? . . ." he repeated, incredulous. "What happened? What did Wexcombe say to you? Damn it, Kit, look at me!"

"I will thank you not to address me in that familiar manner," she said with frosty disdain. "And you need not swear at me."

A stunned look crossed the marquess's handsome face. "Good God. He told you."

She struggled to keep her anguish at bay. "Yes. He told me everything. How he suspected me of being after the dowager's money, and how he asked you to seduce me and ruin me in the dowager's eyes."

"Kit, I can explain."

She laughed, a raw, brittle sound. "A bit late for that, my lord."

"I was going to tell you," he stated grimly.

"Oh? And when were you going to do that? When you had become bored with me and moved on to your next mistress?"

His jaw tightened. "Of course not."

"Then when? No, do not bother; I have already heard enough lies to last a lifetime."

She saw him wince. "It's not like that. Please, listen to me."

Kit turned to face him, her head up. "All right, my lord. Never let it be said that I did not give you a chance to speak in your own defense."

He closed the distance between them, one hand outstretched. "Kit . . ."

She stepped back to avoid his touch. "That is close enough."

"God, how can I? . . . It was never supposed to be like this." Shadows lingered in his dark eyes. "When Wexcombe first came to me and told me about you, my first thought was for Aunt Josephine's safety. But soon after I met you I realized my mistake."

"Then why continue the charade, my lord? Why did you not tell me the truth?"

He sighed and shoved a hand through his hair, rumpling the dark waves. "Because you would have reacted badly. Like you are now."

"That is a paltry excuse."

"I wanted to tell you," he insisted. "But the more I

learned about you, the more attracted to you I became. In the end, I knew I could not insult you so grievously."

"So you strung me along in order to spare my feelings—how noble." Bitterness permeated her words.

"Kit, I had not planned to make you my mistress."

She folded her arms over her chest. "Your persistent attentions seemed to indicate otherwise, as did your infamous proposal."

"I would never have asked you to fulfill your part of that bargain."

"No, you would have continued the seduction until I fell into your bed of my own accord."

A deep flush rose in his face. "Kit, it's not easy for a man to admit that he's been a complete scoundrel."

"A complete scoundrel? Oh, you give yourself far too much credit, my lord," she shot back.

"What would you have done if at the end of the week I had told you that I was wrong to put a price on my assistance, and that we should go our separate ways, with no regrets or obligation?"

"A very easy thing for you to say now, given that the cat is already out of the bag." God, every word he spoke seemed to shred her heart into tiny pieces. Tears pricked her eyes, but she refused to let him see her cry.

His flush intensified. "Kit, not everything was a lie. After the dowager's fall, when you turned to me for comfort . . . that was real."

"Was it?" A sad smile touched her lips, and she reached for her traveling cloak. "Where you are concerned, my lord, I fear I can no longer discern what is real and what is yet another deception."

With a growl, he lunged forward and seized her arms just above the elbow. "Blast it all, Kit! Do not tell me you are indifferent to the passion that lies between us. You have felt it. I know you have. Just this morning you re-sponded to my kisses with a desire that equaled my own."

Kit swallowed around the lump in her throat. "Is pas-sion all you have to offer, my lord?"

"I . . . I do not know. At the moment—yes."

His words snuffed out the last tiny flame of hope. She pulled away. "Then let me go."

He released her, his face set in haggard lines. "Kit, give me another chance. Allow me to make amends."

She shook her head. "No, Lord Bainbridge. You have seduced me, lied to me, and used me in the most abom-inable fashion. I have had enough."

"You can't leave like this," he maintained.

"Can I not? With the exception of the dowager, I see no reason why I should stay."

His hands fell to his sides. "You will not remain, even for her sake?"

"No. She will understand."

His face closed over. "I see. So what do you intend to do now?"

She gulped back her tears and replied, "I am going to return home, my lord. And I am going to forget you."

His body numb, the marquess watched her as she fas-tened her cloak, gathered her reticule, and marched from the room. She did not look back.

He put out one arm and steadied himself against the back of a chair. Dear God. What had he done? All his good intentions had come crashing down around his ears, but he had not expected it to leave him with such a tremendous sense of guilt, pain, and loss.

Go after her, you dolt!

His lips twisted in a sneer. Yes, go after her . . . and then what? Have her reject him yet again? What good would that do? She had made up her mind; that much was obvious. If Katherine Mallory had her way, she would never see him again, and thank God for it.

"Ah, there you are, Bainbridge. Gone, has she?"

The marquess raised his head to see his cousin standing in the doorway, a small, almost smug smile on his narrow face. He stiffened. "Why, Wexcombe?"

"Because it had to be done. I've seen you fascinated by women before, but never like this."

"What you did was reprehensible. You hurt her. Deliberately."

"You managed to do that much on your own, Cousin," the duke replied with a casual shrug. "I simply made her aware of the circumstances."

Bainbridge scowled. "Damn you, I didn't mean for it to end like this. I would have broken it off, with her none the wiser. She didn't have to know. She was innocent."

"Well, she had no designs on Grandmama's money, if that's what you mean. But as for innocent . . . I told you earlier that she was playing for higher stakes."

"You never bothered to talk to her," snapped the marquess, "so how would you know?"

"Because anyone with eyes in his head could see what was going on between the two of you. I do not think you would have broken it off."

Bainbridge grimaced. "I should have done it days ago. It was selfish of me not to."

"You see? So what I did was for your own good."

"My own good?" Bainbridge stalked toward his cousin. "And what would you know of that?"

The duke examined his manicured nails. "If you had not ended it with her, what would you have done?" He paused and peered intently at the marquess. "My God. You weren't actually considering making her an offer of marriage, were you?"

A slow smile stole over Bainbridge's lips as his cousin's words registered in his stunned mind. Marriage . . . to Kit? Only this morning he had thought the notion absurd. But the more he thought about it, the more he recognized the strange sense of longing that gripped him. Kit—his wife. Raising children together, telling stories to them. Having picnics on warm summer days, sharing bowlfuls of strawberries. Having her in his bed night after night for a lifetime. A thrill coursed through him.

"Why not?" he replied.

The duke gaped at him. "Why? . . . Because the woman is a Cit's widow, for God's sake, and the daughter of a social pariah. Suitable as a mistress, perhaps, but as a wife? Preposterous. I swear I don't know what has come over you."

Mistresses . . . He'd had his fill of them. He had spent years pursuing one new lover after another, but none of them had captured his attention for long; all he could remember was a string of faceless bodies. A shallow way of life, in retrospect. Was that all he wanted? The thought of returning to Angelique's vapid blond embrace made him shudder with revulsion. Such an existence may have satisfied him in the past, but now he found he craved something more.

Realization struck him like a thunderbolt. All his life he had derided love for the pain it could bring, never recognizing how much joy he had denied himself in the process. Time for him to follow his own advice: no more running away. Yes; he would do it. At this point, he had nothing to lose.

"What's come over me?" he said softly. "I'll tell you, Cousin. I love her."

The duke snorted. "Don't be ridiculous. You're simply

infatuated with her because she's different from ladies of the *ton*. You will forget about her soon enough."

Bainbridge shook his head, grinning. "You do not understand, do you Wexcombe? This goes beyond infatuation. I think I've finally discovered what I want."

The duke's gaze was cold enough to extinguish burning coals. "No. I will not allow it. You are a marquess, and you have a duty to your family."

"Allow?" Bainbridge scoffed. "I would like to see you try to stop me, Cousin."

"What are you going to do?" the duke demanded.

Bainbridge tugged at his jacket. "Somehow, some way, I am going to win her back. And then I will marry her."

The duke made a dismissive gesture. "I doubt that. She'll never let you near her. Not after all that has happened."

"Perhaps. But I can try."

"Oh, for God's sake, man, don't be a fool," snapped the duke.

The marquess inclined his head in a mocking bow. "Strange that you should say that, Cousin. I've been too great a fool already."

Chapter Ten

*K*it glanced over the rim of her teacup down to the portion of Camden Place visible from the drawing room window. Compared to Calcutta, Bath was a placid, sedate sort of town. No garish colors, no horned cattle meandering down the middle of the road, no vendors hawking their wares with singsong cries, no street performers with cobras or trained monkeys. Here, on an ordinary day, one could see only carriages, pedestrians, and the occasional rider.

But today the streets were more quiet than usual, due to the steady curtain of rain that had fallen since early morning. Raindrops pattered in an even rhythm against the glass, forming a counterpoint to the ticking of the clock on the mantel. Kit sighed and took another sip of hot *chai*, allowing the familiar combination of cinnamon, cloves, and cardamom to dispel the damp chill that had taken hold of her.

After the debacle at Broadwell Manor, part of her had been tempted to bolt pell-mell back to India, but she knew the notion was pure fantasy. Besides, she did not want to give *him* the satisfaction of seeing her run. Moreover, in the past fortnight she had discovered that Bath had a quiet charm of its own, which at the moment she found particularly appealing. This was her home, and she refused to be driven away.

Fortunately, it had not come to that; the marquess had not followed her to Bath. Oh, not that she wanted him to, of course, or even expected it. In fact, she hoped never to see his roguish countenance ever again. Two weeks had blunted the worst of her pain, but every time she thought about it, she knew, despite her defiant words, that forgetting Lord Bainbridge would take much, much longer.

With a shake of her head, Kit set down her cup and picked up the latest letter from the dowager duchess. When the missive arrived this morning, just as she was preparing to go out, she had broken the seal and scanned the contents immediately. But once she had assured herself that the elderly woman's health had not taken a turn for the worse, she had set it aside so that she might savor it later. Now she unfolded the letter, smoothed the creased parchment sheets, and retraced the words written in the dowager's familiar, spiky lettering.

The dowager continued to recover well, it seemed, and was driving everyone at Broadwell Manor, especially the duke, to distraction with her demands. A smile quirked the corners of Kit's mouth. The dowager, as ever, was in fine form. Ah, but here was something—

> *I have also heard reports from several of my acquaintances that you have been cutting quite a dash at the new Assembly Rooms. Good for you, child! 'Tis high time you put aside your nunnish ways. At any rate, I should hate to think my letters of introduction had gone to waste.*

Kit grinned. She had only been to two balls, but apparently her appearance had caused enough of a stir for the dowager's friends to remark upon it. At this time of year, most of the *ton* were either at their country estates or in Brighton; the population of Bath, it seemed, was comprised mostly of dowagers, widows, half-pay officers, young girls wishing to live down a recent scandal, and fortune hunters down on their luck. In such company, Kit supposed, she could not help but stand out. But there was more. . . .

Lady Arbogast went so far as to relate that a certain group of gentlemen—and she was not too particular about the term—have taken to calling you "The Maharani of Bath." You must write to me at once, child, and tell me what you have done to merit such a tantalizing epithet. Oh, how vexed I am to think that I am missing all of this!

Kit made a moue. "The Maharani of Bath," indeed. That made it sound like she was parading about the city on the back of an elephant, or in a palanquin at the very least, festooned with pearls and rubies and diamonds and accompanied by dozens of handmaidens wielding gigantic peacock-feather fans. She snorted. What a ridiculous notion!

In truth, all she had done was have her mantua-maker create a new wardrobe from several silk saris she had collected during her years in India. Well, come to think of it, she had also unpacked several pieces of elaborate, wrought-gold jewelry and her embroidered, curl-toed slippers. Hmm. She had worn these things without a second thought in India, but apparently such attire had made more of an impression on staid Bath than she had expected.

She was fairly certain she knew who had coined that ridiculous soubriquet: Viscount Langley, who during the last week had worked himself to the forefront of her admirers. Although she had met him but a few days ago, she had the impression that he was a handsome young rascal with a flair for the dramatic.

But you had best remain guarded, my dear, for such notoriety will garner you more than your share of attention, not all of it wanted.

Kit's smile began to fade. Wise advice, indeed. Most of the men who had flocked to her side over the past week were fortune hunters, drawn by her silk gowns and rich jewelry—signs that marked her as a wealthy widow. Her chin came up. She must remember to tell the dowager that her concern was appreciated but entirely unnecessary; she was no longer the naïve, trusting little idiot she had been a month ago. Her mouth firmed, and she continued to read.

Once you decide what you want, child, there is no going back. There are plenty of fine young men to be had for the asking; all that remains is for you to find one—or for one to find you.

Kit rolled her eyes. After what had happened at Broadwell Manor, the dowager had somehow gotten the idea into her head that Kit needed to remarry. The elderly woman would not take kindly to being contradicted, but Kit suspected she would have to do it sooner, rather than later. She shrugged and kept reading.

*I hope to be able to join you in Bath very soon.
Wexcombe's physician—who is not the quack for
which I first mistook him—has pronounced me in
excellent health, and said that I will be fit for travel
in a few days. And not before time, I shouldn't wonder. Although the children have been absolute an-
gels, I believe everyone else here at Broadwell shall
be delighted to see me leave, and I, for one, cannot
wait to oblige them.*

Kit read down to the signature, then set the letter aside
and smiled. The duke would be more than happy to see
his grandmother leave, and it served him right.

She poured herself another cup of *chai* and returned to
the window, watching individual rivulets of water glide
downward and merge with others on the pane. Since the
dowager would not be able to return to Bath for a while,
Kit determined to send the elderly woman another letter
to tide her over. She glanced toward her rosewood escritoire, then to the mantel clock. No, she had better wait
until tomorrow morning. Her smile melded with the rim
of her cup as she sipped the spicy, steaming *chai*. She had
promised Viscount Langley a dance at this evening's ball,
and she was certain the dowager would not forgive her if
she failed to describe, in very thorough detail, what was
sure to be another very interesting evening.

Lord Bainbridge tamped down a surge of irritation as
his carriage inched through traffic along Alfred Street.
This was Bath, by Lucifer's beard, not Pall Mall! What
the devil were all these people doing out and about at six
o'clock in the evening? It had taken him most of the afternoon to learn that Kit would be at the Upper Assembly

Rooms tonight—but so, apparently, was everyone else in Bath.

The carriage ground to a halt once more; the marquess heard muffled shouts of anger and the whinnying of horses from up the street. More delays. Blast it! Two weeks he'd waited. Two long weeks. He *would* see her. Tonight.

With a muttered oath, the marquess threw open the door, called a few instructions to his bewildered coachman, then loped off down the street, shoulders hunched against the steady rain, pulling his curly brimmed beaver farther down onto his brow.

He should not have waited so long. When Kit had left Broadwell Manor, his first instinct had been to run after her, to kiss her senseless . . . or at least until she agreed to listen to reason. Then he had determined that it was better to let her anger cool a bit before he approached her again, so he had traveled posthaste back to London and tied up his affairs there.

Or, he should say rather, *affaires*. Angelique had sobbed in the most brokenhearted manner when he'd given her her *congé*, but the diamond bracelet he had purchased for her at Rundell and Bridge had dammed the flow in a remarkably short time.

Then his most irrational move: he had ridden to Bainbridge Hall in Yorkshire. After all, if he was going to marry, he wanted to bring his bride . . . he wanted to bring Kit home.

That had proved to be his undoing.

His years as an absentee landlord had caught up with him; the house in which he had grown up showed obvious signs of neglect. Even now, pangs of guilt jabbed him just thinking about it. Some things remained untouched, like the carved stone staircase that arched up to the first floor and the ornate plasterwork on the walls, but half the chimneys now leaned at dangerous angles, window frames showed signs of rot, and the rose garden had become a veritable jungle of weeds. His mother's garden. He and Geoffrey had pretended to be King Arthur and Lancelot along those intertwined paths and around the hedges while his mother smiled and worked among the roses. Such memories . . .

In trying to run away from all the nightmares he associated with the house, he had forgotten almost everything pleasant. Despite all that had happened, this was still home. Bainbridge cursed himself for a fool. All these years spent in pursuit of pleasure had blinded him to the needs of the house and his tenants. Wexcombe was right—he *was* a selfish bastard, but not, he hoped, an irredeemable one.

One look at the accounts told him all he needed to know; he summarily sacked Dunning, the shifty-eyed troll who had also served as his father's estate manager, and hired a local man, Cavendish, in his place. Before he realized it he had stayed another week, working with the new steward to oversee the start of renovations. He directed Cavendish to begin with the restoration of the Queen's Chamber. After all, he couldn't ask Kit to stay in rooms with moth-eaten bed hangings and peeling wallpaper.

So much was left to be done, but his instincts clamored at him to return; he had let too much time elapse already. Once he was assured that everything was properly underway at the Hall, he had returned to London, and from there to Bath.

His prolonged travel had given him time to think, to form a plan to win Kit back. Now that she'd had ample time to cool her temper, he could apologize in earnest.

Apologize, and assure her that his intentions had never been as black as Wexcombe painted them to be. Kit was one of the most rational females of his acquaintance; then again, he had hurt her deeply, and reason held little sway where wounded emotions were concerned. She might refuse him admittance to her house, but odds were she would not cut him in public. He would be better served to meet with her in the Assembly Rooms first.

He allowed himself a grin as he hastened down the darkened streets of Bath, even with rain dripping from the brim of his hat, down his cape, and into his evening pumps. She had not gone to ground, as he feared she might. Her presence at the new Assembly Rooms indicated that she had followed his counsel and had stopped hiding behind her books. Had she stopped hiding beneath those tentlike gowns, as well?

His grin broadened with anticipation. He had won her over once before, and he had not even used all his charm to do it. Surely he was more than ready for this second challenge.

When the marquess reached the octagonal vestibule of the Upper Rooms, he was amazed at the crowd gathered there. He managed to divest himself of his hat and cape, then used his height to advantage as he waded through the assembled throng. Lud, every single dowager and country squire in Bath must have taken up residence here tonight. Snippets of conversation reached his ears:

". . . decked out like an Eastern princess. How vulgar."

"Hmph. Holding court like one, too, I daresay."

". . . unusual-looking chit. Not exactly pretty, is she?"

". . . admit anyone these days. A Cit's widow, 'pon rep!"

Bainbridge's ears pricked up. Kit. They had to be talking about Kit. His heart accelerated a bit as he came to the doorway of the ballroom.

He had no trouble spotting her amid the multitude. Bathed in light from the five chandeliers, she glowed like a sun-kissed pearl. He made his way toward her, his heart clenched in his chest. Dear God, she was beautiful. Rather than the drab frocks she'd worn before, she was now dressed in an exquisite creation of deep peach silk shot through with gold threads. Bands of intricate, raised-gold embroidery trimmed the sleeves, hem, waist, and the temptingly rounded neckline. The cut of the gown emphasized the length of her neck and the slender span of her waist. Strands of pearl-trimmed ribbon decorated her upswept hair, and an exotic necklace of gold and pearls adorned her throat. Gold bracelets jingled on her wrists as she cooled herself with a carved sandalwood fan. He swallowed hard as a wave of heat swept over him.

But as he drew nearer, he noticed a large number of men gathered around her, and that quickly cooled his blazing desire. He recognized a few, for their reputations preceded them: Sir Henry Castleton, a dissipated roué who had buried two wives already and was apparently in the market for a third. Lord Tarlton, who was at least fifty if he was day, and who had just last month lost a fortune at White's hazard table. Lord Edward Mitton, who had squandered his inheritance by the time he was twenty and had sponged off his dwindling circle of friends ever since. Viscount Langley, an inveterate gamester who had won and lost fortunes on the flip of a card.

Some of the others did not seem so objectionable, like Lieutenant the Honorable Wilfred Oddingley-Smythe, an infantry officer who had been wounded at Salamanca, and Sir Percival Debenham, whose only failing was his

youth—the boy was barely old enough to shave, much
less court a widow six years his senior.

None of them should prove to be much trouble . . . except Langley, perhaps. Kit had just turned her head and
laughed at something the viscount had said. Hearing that
throaty laugh and knowing it was meant for someone else
made Bainbridge grit his teeth so hard that his jaw ached.
Time to get her away from this gallery of rogues.

He elbowed his way into Kit's circle of admirers. She
turned; their gazes met. Her green eyes widened.

"Hello, Kit," said Bainbridge.

Kit's breath froze in her lungs. Oh, sweet heaven—he
was here.

Here, and more devastatingly handsome than ever in
his elegant black and white evening dress. A diamond
twinkled at her from the intricate folds of his snowy cravat, its hard glitter matching that of the marquess's eyes.
A shiver cascaded down the length of her spine.

"Lord Bainbridge," she replied, her voice high and
breathy. "What brings you to Bath?"

He inclined his head to her, a slight smile on his lips.
"I think you know."

"Bainbridge!" exclaimed Lord Langley with a bit too
much jovial enthusiasm. "How odd that we should see
you here. I thought Bath would be too dull for your
taste."

"That only proves how little you know me," Bainbridge murmured in reply.

From the alcove above, the musicians started up with
an allemande. The marquess turned to her. "May I have
this dance, Mrs. Mallory?"

Kit's heart leaped into her throat, but before she could
reply Lord Langley reached out and took her gloved
hand.

"You must get in line, Bainbridge," the viscount stated. "The lady has promised this dance to me."

Bainbridge looked to her. "Kit?"

Though her pulse pounded in her ears, she managed to lift her chin and stare haughtily back at him. How dare he march in here and expect her to jump at his command! She favored the viscount with a cool smile. "You are quite right, Lord Langley. This is indeed your dance."

The satisfaction of watching the marquess's face darken with anger dissipated as soon as the viscount guided her out onto the dance floor.

"Are you well, Mrs. Mallory?" Langley asked in low tones.

"Yes, my lord. Fit as a fiddle. Why do you ask?"

He raised one golden brown brow. "Because, dear lady, you have gone quite pale."

Kit raised a gloved hand to her cheek. "I have?"

"If you prefer to sit out this dance, I would gladly fetch you a glass of lemonade."

She flashed him a grateful look. "No, my lord, but I do appreciate your offer."

Langley glanced over his shoulder. "If I may hazard a guess without being thought impertinent, might I conclude that Lord Bainbridge is the source of your distress?"

Her jaw tightened. "You might."

"Should I call him out?"

Kit stared at him, only to notice the teasing glint in his slate blue eyes. "No violence on my behalf, my lord, I beg you."

"Ah." He gave her hand a gentle squeeze. "Very well, Mrs. Mallory. But I shall do my best to see that he does not distress you again this evening."

Kit did not have a chance to reply, for the dance had

begun, and soon she and the viscount were too caught up in the figures to hold much of a conversation. Although Lord Langley proved to be a diverting dance partner, she could not shake the feeling that Bainbridge's eyes lingered on her wherever she went.

When the allemande ended, Sir Percy claimed her for a country dance, and Lord Tarlton for the reel after that. But when Sir Henry Castleton tried to solicit her hand, she pleaded fatigue and begged to sit out the dance. The baronet appeared displeased, but did not press the issue, for which Kit was infinitely grateful. She did not like the older man; he did not bother to disguise his leering glances, and his clammy, reptilian touch never failed to make her shudder.

It was rather like being part of a circus, only she was one of the performers; she wasn't sure if she liked the sensation. On one hand, being watched and admired was rather flattering, but as the dowager had said in her letter, not all the attention was entirely welcome.

Like that of Lord Bainbridge.

The crowd in the Assembly Rooms had noticed the marquess's presence by now; the air hummed with murmured speculation. Kit guessed that a man of Lord Bainbridge's stature—and rakish reputation—was rarely seen in Bath. He stood at the edge of the room, elegant as ever, seemingly oblivious to the whispered furor around him, and equally unaware of the longing looks sent his way by several young ladies.

As Kit returned to her chair, she saw his head swivel in her direction. Her lips thinned. So much for hoping to stay unnoticed.

Lord Langley appeared at her elbow. "May I be of some assistance, Mrs. Mallory?" he asked softly.

Kit tried to smile. "No, thank you, my lord. I have to face this sooner or later; I cannot run forever."

"I shall not be far, if you have need of me," he said, bowing over her hand.

"Will you excuse us a moment, Langley?" inquired the marquess. His words were polite, but Kit heard the quiet length of steel running through them.

"Of course, my lord," Langley drawled. "But I shall not let you monopolize her for long. Would you care for a glass of lemonade, Mrs. Mallory?"

The viscount was giving her an opportunity for a gracious exit, should she need it. She nodded. "Yes, thank you."

"Then I shall return shortly." Langley shot the marquess a warning look, then vanished into the crowd.

Kit snapped open her sandalwood fan and fanned herself at what she hoped was a leisurely pace. Her whole body felt as though it would shake apart at any moment. Fortunately, her long skirts hid her quaking limbs.

"What do you think you are doing, my lord?" she demanded.

A muscle twitched at his temple. "You know why I'm here, Kit."

"I do not," she countered. "Perhaps you should enlighten me."

He sighed. "Kit, I came here to apologize. I never meant to hurt you, and I think you know that."

Several people nearby turned their heads, their expressions full of unseemly curiosity. Kit felt her face redden. "This is neither the time nor the place for such a private discussion, sir."

The musicians launched into a stately minuet; Bainbridge seized her hand and began to lead her onto the dance floor. "Then this should allow us some privacy."

"What? How dare you!" Kit hissed, hoping no one would overhear.

The marquess gave her one of his roguish, heart-stopping smiles. "I dare, sweet Kit, because you leave me no other choice."

A formal court dance of the previous century, the minuet was excruciating under the best of circumstances. Tonight, Kit found it to be nothing less than torture. Though separated by layers of kidskin, she could still feel the warmth of his hand upon hers. And his eyes . . . Those dark, seductive orbs seemed to follow every move she made.

"Very well, my lord, I accept your apology," she murmured as they passed through a set of figures. "Now you can return to London with a clear conscience, if you indeed possess such a thing."

The marquess's eyes narrowed. "I do not plan to return to London, Kit."

She feigned innocence. "Oh? Do you intend to stay and take the waters, then? I have heard they are quite beneficial to one's health."

Irritation flashed over his face. "I am not leaving here without you."

She uttered a rather unladylike snort. "Then I fear you will be in Bath a very long time, sir, because I have no intention of going anywhere, especially with you."

"Then I will wait."

She stumbled; he caught her against him. Her silk-clad thigh and hip made contact with his, and a jolt of electricity surged through her. Heat flooded her face. She drew back to keep a more decorous distance between them.

"You see?" he said with an infuriatingly smug smile. "You cannot deny the attraction between us."

"The only thing between us, my lord," she muttered under her breath, "is an abominable history of lies and deception."

"I was going to tell you the truth," he insisted, "but Wexcombe stole a march on me with his untimely revelation."

"You say that as if it excuses your conduct!" she snapped. The elderly couple dancing next to them glanced at her with patent disapproval, but she paid little heed. "What you and your cousin did was despicable, my lord. And if you think for one moment that flattery and insincere apologies will get you what you want, then you are greatly mistaken."

Putting his arm around her waist, the marquess guided her off the dance floor and around the edge of the room, where the crowd had thinned somewhat. "And what do you think I want?"

Her body reacted to the pure seductiveness in his voice and his touch; longing pooled deep within her. She tried to ignore it. "I . . . You know what I think."

"You did not answer my question." His dark eyes glinted. He was enjoying this!

She glared back. "Very well. I will make myself perfectly clear on this point, my lord, so there can be no further doubt. I will not be your mistress. Ever."

He quirked an eyebrow. "Do you think me such a villain?"

"Yes."

Bainbridge raised her fingers to his lips with a teasing smile. "And yet you cannot deny that you are fond of me."

Pain began to throb at Kit's temples. "If this is your idea of a joke, my lord—"

"Nicholas," he amended with a smile. "Remember?"

He turned her hand over and stroked his thumb along her gloved wrist.

Kit shivered. The pain in her head increased to a pounding. "I am through playing these games with you, sirrah," she declared. She snatched back her hand and glared at him. "And I will thank you to leave me alone." Spinning on her heel, she gathered her skirts and stalked in the opposite direction.

"Kit, wait!" he called after her. "That's not what I —" The rest of his words were swallowed by the crowd.

Damn him. *Damn him!*

Tears misted Kit's vision as she fought her way toward the octagonal vestibule. Curious eyes probed at her from every direction; she raised her head, determined to maintain what remained of her composure.

After all that he had done, how could he simply walk back into her life and attempt to resume their relationship as though nothing had happened? For him to tantalize her in such an outrageous manner . . . and in public? The man had no moral character, no scruples at all, and she was well rid of him.

If only her body did not ache so very badly for his touch.

Viscount Langley intercepted her at the doorway, his handsome face distorted with worry. "Are you all right, Mrs. Mallory?"

Kit shook her head. "Would . . . would you be so good as to see me home, my lord? The heat . . . I feel a trifle faint."

Langley nodded and offered her his arm. "Of course; it would be my pleasure." Then, in a lower voice, he added, "If that bounder upset you, you have but to say the word, and I will call him out."

Her eyes widened with alarm. "No! Please, my lord,

no more talk of dueling. As much as I appreciate your ve-
hemence on my behalf, I assure you that all I need is to
get well away from the Marquess of Bainbridge."

Lord Langley gave her a lopsided smile. "I may be
only a viscount, Mrs. Mallory, and a rather impoverished
one at that, but may I be so bold as to offer you my company as a potential diversion from his presence?"

Moisture gleamed on the edges of Kit's lashes. He was
a handsome young man, though not as handsome as
Nicholas—as Lord Bainbridge. His golden brown hair
brightened toward blond at the crown, testament to a
great deal of time spent out-of-doors. His tanned skin emphasized the blue of his eyes and his gleaming white
teeth. He was not as tall as Ni—as Lord Bainbridge, nor
were his shoulders quite as broad, but he was attractive,
he was kind, and he was not a rake.

She swallowed her tears. "You may, my lord, but only
if you promise never to lie to me."

The skin around Langley's eyes crinkled as his smile
widened. He raised her fingers to his lips. "Dear lady, I
would do anything you asked."

Chapter Eleven

*B*ainbridge paced the length of his room, turned, and paced back.

Damn.

He'd rushed his fences last night, and his rashness may have set him back even further. Instead of paying respectful and serious attention to Kit, he had behaved as he always did around members of the fairer sex. Just as at Broadwell Manor, he had found himself flirting with her, teasing her.

Seducing her.

Damn!

Was that the only way he knew how to relate to a woman?

For God's sake, stop being provoking and just tell her!

Weariness weighted his eyelids, but he had no time to heed the siren song of sleep. He thrust a hand through his hair. Think. He had to think. He had tried to follow Kit last night to explain, but Langley, that insolent pup, had intercepted Kit and spirited her away. Bad enough that he'd put his foot in it, but if he wasn't careful, Langley would take advantage of the situation more than he already had; the thought of playing into a rival's hands galled him to no end.

Perhaps he had been mistaken in seeking her out at the Assembly Rooms, after all. But would she receive him if he called upon her? Pulling a face, he bellowed first for his valet, then for coffee. He would have to risk it. So much for foolproof plans!

Bainbridge dressed with painstaking care, then left the White Hart for Camden Place. The rain had ceased overnight, and bright late-morning sunshine glinted off the numerous puddles in the cobbled streets. He winced and lowered the shade over the carriage window.

Lud, he had never worked himself into such a state before. No sleep, and less appetite. All this over a woman. His lips stretched in a gesture that was more grimace than grin. If anyone had told him that love for a lady would bring him to such a state, he would have laughed outright. As it was, every single nerve in his body seemed to be stretched to the limit, like a drawn bowstring. A knot of tension had gathered across his shoulders and showed no signs of lessening.

She would see him. She must.

The carriage brought him to Camden Place in short order, only to have Kit's tall, rather imposing Hindu butler inform him that the *memsahib* was not in, but due to return at any moment. His heart leaped; dare he hope? Assuming a businesslike air, Bainbridge presented his card and asked to wait for her. The servant eyed him with undisguised suspicion, weighing his merits, then bowed and admitted him to the drawing room.

The marquess's eyes widened as he surveyed his surroundings. Incense scented the air. Stone statues of what appeared to be half-naked dancing goddesses graced either side of the fireplace. Leering masks, some human, some distinctly animal, regarded him from above the mantelpiece. And then there was the large bronze fellow in the vestibule. . . .

This was Kit's world. Her home. Bainbridge crossed the room to admire a carved stone statue, this one of an elephant-headed god with four arms. Despite her unhappiness with her marriage, she had loved India. Loved it so much that she had brought these pieces of it home with her. He caressed the elephant's cool stone trunk. How it must have pained her to leave.

How much did he really know about her? Not enough . . . not nearly enough. He wanted to know everything, wanted to hear her stories. Perhaps, like Scheherazade, she would tell him one story night after night, so that he might forever discover something new about her. He smiled to himself.

But his smile faded as the minutes ticked by. Where could she be? He shot an impatient glance at the mantel clock, then began to pace back and forth over the tiger-skin rug. The Hindu butler offered him tea, but he declined. At this rate, brandy or blue ruin were the only things that would settle him, and he didn't want to declare himself to Kit when he was half disguised. His reputation with her was besmirched enough already.

Twenty minutes later, Bainbridge heard the front door open, heard her voice. He stopped midpace and clasped his hands behind his back, his jaw tight. Lud, it would not do for her to see him behaving like some impatient, lovestruck schoolboy.

The butler must have informed her of his presence; Bainbridge heard a sharp "What?", followed by a rapid flurry of words in a foreign language. He grimaced. No, she was not pleased to see him. He should have expected as much.

Kit appeared in the drawing room doorway, her green eyes ablaze with fury, her cheeks flushed. His throat tightened. God, she was magnificent.

"What are you doing here?" she demanded. "I thought I asked you to leave me alone."

"Forgive me," he hastened to say. "I made a mull of things last night. Ordinarily I would never think to invade your privacy like this, but I had to see you—to apologize, and to explain."

From the thunderous expression on her face, Bainbridge feared for a moment that she was about to order her servants to throw him out. "There is nothing to explain, my lord," she snapped. "Your actions last evening made your intentions perfectly clear. I will thank you to leave my house at once!"

He held up a hand. "If you send me away, Kit, you will never know the truth."

"The truth?" Her golden brows arched skyward. "The truth is that you take nearly every opportunity to seduce me, sir, and I refuse to expose myself to such low and callous behavior."

"I do get rather carried away when I am with you," he confessed. "But in doing so I caused you undue distress, and for that I apologize."

She hesitated. "You have become quite proficient at apologies, my lord."

"So it would seem." He shifted uneasily on the tigerskin rug.

"Neither of us would be in this situation if you had respected my wishes in the first place and simply left me alone."

"You tempt me to madness, Kit."

"Then you should be in Bedlam, sir."

"I shall be, if you do not hear me out."

She sighed, then glided slowly into the room. "Oh, very well." Beneath her breath, she added, "I do not know why on earth I am agreeing to this."

He attempted a smile. "Because you have soft spot for irrepressible rogues?"

"That, or I am the one who belongs in Bedlam."

"This is a madness that affects us both," he murmured.

She stared at him a moment, her eyes cool chips of jade. Only the rapid rise and fall of her breasts betrayed any hint of alarm. "I would not be so sure of that." She gestured to a chair. "Won't you sit down?"

He ran a hand through his hair, rumpling the waves his valet had so carefully arranged only a few hours before. "No, thank you." He did not trust himself to sit still.

"As you wish." Graceful as ever, she smoothed the skirts of her moss-colored morning gown and lowered herself into a claw-footed chair. She laced her fingers in her lap and gazed at him with wary eyes. "I am waiting, my lord."

Heat washed over the back of his neck, but he resisted the urge to rub at it. Good God, how could a man so glib with compliments and flattery be so suddenly tongue-tied? He blew out his breath in a gusty sigh. "I did not come to Bath to ask you to be my mistress."

Her eyes widened, then narrowed. "Oh? Your behavior at the Assembly Rooms gave me quite the opposite impression." She rubbed her thumb across one wrist; Bainbridge realized that was where he had touched her last night.

"I meant to draw you aside and ask for permission to call on you, but, as has happened too often of late, my best intentions went awry."

"Indeed."

Bainbridge paced over to the statue of the elephant

god. "I saw all those reprobates flirting with you and . . ." He ran a hand down the stone trunk. "I did something I have never done in recent memory: I lost my head."

Kit pursed her lips. "Oh? I did not discern a noticeable difference in your conduct, my lord. Whether jealous, angry, or indifferent, you always seem to treat a woman as though you want to seduce her."

Touché. He grimaced. "I did not realize that until recently. Women have . . . responded to me ever since I was young, and it did not take me long to realize that I could, in turn, use my charm to get what I wanted from them."

A dull flush rose in her face. "Apparently that approach has proven quite effective."

"Yes. But I cannot use it to get what I truly want."

She straightened, her eyes round. "What do you mean?"

Bainbridge rubbed his chin, feeling the slight burn of razor-nicked skin. "I was wrong not to have broken off our rather imprudent relationship, Kit. I freely admit that. Part of me did not want to hurt you, but the other part wanted to continue in blissful ignorance, enjoying your companionship and your kisses."

Her flush deepened. She plucked at the fabric of her skirt.

"I craved your company," he continued, "but at the time I thought myself drawn to you because you were different from other women I had known. You possess this strange combination of exoticism and innocence, Kit, and I had never encountered that before. You intrigued me, and I found myself wanting to know more about you, to get past that drab shell you presented to the world and discover what was beneath. And the more I knew, the more attracted I became. My baser nature wanted nothing more than for you to be my mistress."

"Stop," she whispered.

"You need to hear everything, Kit, if you wish to understand."

She squeezed her eyes shut, bit her lip, then nodded. "All right. Go on."

"Only after you left Broadwell did I realize what I wanted—and it had nothing to do with mistresses."

Her eyes flew open. "What, then?"

Bainbridge paced across the tiger skin toward her, his shoulders taut. "I have been a selfish creature most of my life, Kit. Always remaining aloof, but still willing to take advantage of the pleasures women offered to me. But this time . . ." He turned to face her, pinning her with an intent stare. "I want something more. I want summer picnics beneath the trees. Stories replete with princes and demons. Bowlfuls of strawberries. Children."

She looked up at him with huge eyes. All traces of color drained from her complexion.

"Kit." The marquess took her hands and pulled her from her chair. "I want you to marry me. Be my wife."

Kit clutched Lord Bainbridge's strong hands as the room seemed to spin around her in a most disconcerting fashion. "Your . . . wife?" she echoed.

His mouth quirked in a half smile. "Do you find the concept so strange?"

"Only when it comes from you, my lord." Kit pulled back and tried to ignore the way the smile slid from Lord Bainbridge's face.

"That is why I followed you to Bath," he insisted. He held fast to her hands. "That is why I insisted on speaking with you. Marry me, Kit. Marry me, and make me the happiest man in England."

She disengaged herself from his grasp and sidled over

to the window. Her stomach churned. "But would you be?"

He frowned. "What sort of a question is that?"

She licked her dry lips. "Would you be happy?"

"I just told you—"

"But you must admit this is a rather sudden change of heart. . . ." Her voice trailed off in a whisper.

"Is it that I am a rake, and you think me unable to settle down?"

"That is part of it, my lord."

"Nicholas," he prompted in a soft voice.

She shook her head. "No, my lord, I think it more prudent if I maintain at least the illusion of formality between us."

"Kit, tell me what is wrong." His velvet brown eyes pleaded with her.

She clenched her fingers in the folds of her skirt to still their trembling. "I cannot marry you."

Shock drained all color from his handsome features. "Kit, I just told you that I want you above all other women to be my wife and the mother of my children. I want *you*."

Calm, she must be calm about this, even though her heart was beating like the wings of a caged bird. She swallowed hard. "I am very flattered, my lord, but I still cannot marry you."

His nostrils flared; his dark eyes turned from pleading to piercing. "You can at least tell me why."

Kit wrapped her arms around her body. "You once told me that, when you married, you would choose a well-bred lady who held not one ounce of affection for you."

His hands flexed into fists. "That was before I fell in love with you."

Sweet heaven! Tears formed a lump at the back of her

throat. "I thought love was an unnecessary complication."

He strode over and seized her by the shoulders. "By all that's holy, Kit, stop throwing my words back in my face. Don't you understand? I love you."

I love you.

Oh, how she had longed to hear that phrase, first from her father, then from her husband. And now they had come from a man she was not sure she could trust.

He ran a gentle finger down the length of her jaw. She shivered.

"I love you," he repeated, "and I think you love me. You would not have run away from me so quickly if you did not. You loved me, and I hurt you, so you fled."

"I was very foolish to have gotten involved with you," she said, her voice wavering with emotion.

"Kit." He drew her closer to him. "Why do you torture me like this?"

She placed her hands on his chest and tried to push herself away. "This is a farce, my lord. Please let me go."

He did not release her. "No. Do you love me?"

She turned away. She could not escape. "Yes."

"Then marry me." The marquess turned her to face him, leaned down, and brushed his lips over hers. His hands slid down her back and over her waist. "You know how good it would be between us. I love you, Kit. I want you in my bed night after night."

Kit moaned. Oh, how she had longed for his touch, his kiss, the sensation of his body against hers. At this moment she wanted nothing more than to surrender, to give in to this passionate embrace. . . .

A warning sounded at the back of her mind, faint but insistent.

How many other women had succumbed to his sweet

words and tender caresses? Done whatever he wanted for
the promise of pleasure? She had nearly fallen into this
trap once; she would not do so again.

Anger flared hot within her; she shoved at his chest,
then wrenched herself from his arms. "I cannot believe
you would stoop to this! You simply march into my
home, declare your undying love, ply me with a few
kisses, and expect me to fall at your feet? You have not
changed in the least, my lord; you still do not hesitate to
employ seduction to bend a woman to your will."

Storm clouds gathered on Lord Bainbridge's brow.
"Kit, what do you want from me?"

Her hands shook, but she no longer bothered to hide it.
"I suppose I want something that you cannot give me."

"What—love?" he demanded. "I have already told you
I love you, and that is something I have never said to another woman. What more do you want?"

"Trust," she said.

He stared at her, his forehead furrowed in confusion.

She stood in the middle of the drawing room, her body
stiff, her hands balled into fists at her sides. A tear escaped her control and glided in a wet trail down her
cheek; she brushed it away with impatient fingers. "You
deceived me, Nicholas. And yes, you hurt me. Deeply.
But even more than that, you destroyed the trust I had in
you.

"And now you come here and ask me to marry you,
and either you do not believe I know my own mind, or
you fear I will refuse you, so you attempt to seduce me
into accepting you." She shook her head. Another
teardrop joined the first. "Love requires trust, my lord.
And without it, there can be nothing between us."

He reached out a hand to her, then let it fall. "I love

you, Kit," he said, his voice raw. "You love me. I thought that was all we needed to be happy."

"Happy?" She blinked furiously against the onslaught of her tears. "How could I be happy wondering if my husband just came from another woman's bed?"

"I have broken it off with my mistress," he replied with a growl. "I did that two weeks ago, directly after you left Broadwell. I do not want a paramour, Kit; I want you. How many times do I have to say it?"

"How can I be happy wondering if every kiss, every tender touch did not have some secret design behind it?"

His jaw tightened. "Is that all you think me capable of?"

"You came to Bath for the purpose of courting me, did you not?" she countered.

He blinked. "Well . . . yes."

"Ordinarily, my lord, when a gentleman courts a lady he sends her flowers or *billets-doux*. He does not hound her every step and seek to subvert her disdain for him with kisses and seductive banter."

The marquess scowled. "You used to find my kisses and seductive banter appealing."

"So would any woman, my lord. But the fact that you use them indiscriminately tells me that I am nothing special to you."

His shoulders slumped. "Where does that leave us?" he asked quietly.

How tired he looked. More than tired . . . exhausted. Lines of weariness pulled at his mouth; shadows smudged the skin beneath his dark eyes. Kit resisted the urge to reach up and smooth away the lock of black hair that had fallen over his forehead.

"I do not know." She turned away. "Go back to London, my lord. Find a lady who does not love you and marry her instead."

"If I do, both of us will be miserable," he stated. "Kit, how can I prove that you can trust me?"

She nibbled at her lower lip. "I cannot say."

A strange expression crossed Lord Bainbridge's face. "Would you marry me if I could?"

She regarded him with open skepticism. "Yes, but how can one quantify such a thing as trust?"

He walked slowly over to her, took her hands in his, and held them. No teasing, no surreptitious brushing of his fingers over her wrist. Just his strong hands enveloping her smaller ones. "Let me make you a bargain, then."

Kit's eyes widened, and the floor seemed to drop away beneath her. "Oh, no." She tried to pull away. "Not another one. I am not as jingle-brained as all that!"

He did not release her. "Hear me out. Please."

Kit swallowed around her suddenly dry tongue. "What . . . what sort of bargain?"

"A very simple one, actually." He gazed down at her, his eyes like pools of chocolate. "Give me until the end of the week to prove myself worthy of your trust. If I succeed, you consent to be my wife. If not, I shall return to London and never darken your door again."

She stared at him. "Can you possibly be serious about this?"

"I assure you I am in earnest," he replied. "You will have nothing to lose except a week of your time. So . . . what say you?"

"Only that this is utterly ridiculous!" she exclaimed.

"Is it? Remember, you will be the final judge on the matter, since it is your trust I must win. We have a chance to be happy, Kit. Are you willing to take that risk?"

A large, heavy knot gathered in the depths of her stomach. So much of her wanted to hide away from the anguish, from the hurt this could bring. He said she had nothing to lose except her time, but potentially she could lose much, much more. Like her heart. Again.

Her lips compressed. No. She would not run from this. If she denied herself this chance, she may as well lock herself away in a cloister.

"One week?" she asked, hesitant.

He nodded. "One week."

She took a deep, shuddery breath. "Very well, my lord. I agree."

A tired smile crossed his features; he gave her hands a gentle squeeze. "Then I shall ensure that you do not regret it."

"When do we begin?" she asked.

"Seeing that I have only a week, I should make the most of my time." He pondered a moment. "Would you care to take a stroll with me this afternoon?"

Kit started. "A stroll?"

"That *is* an acceptable form of diversion, I hope?" he inquired, not entirely facetiously.

She blushed. "It is, my lord, but I am engaged to drive with Viscount Langley this afternoon."

"Langley." He frowned. "Be careful with that one, Kit. He is reputed to be an irredeemable gamester."

"Just as you are reputed to be an irredeemable rake?"

"Touché, madam," he replied with a growl.

Her blush felt like it extended all the way up to her hairline as she hastened to add, "There is, however, a concert of Italian music to be given this evening at the Assembly Rooms. If you would care to accompany me, of course."

He arched an elegant eyebrow. "I would indeed, Mrs. Mallory. I shall call for you at six."

"I shall be ready, sir," she replied somewhat breath-lessly.

"Until tonight, then." The marquess took her hand and bowed over it. She halfway expected him to flout convention yet again and kiss her fingers, but he kept a very polite distance between her fingertips and his lips. In a way, she was almost disappointed.

He then took his leave; Kit watched from the drawing room window as he sauntered down the townhouse stairs, his hat perched atop his head at a jaunty angle. At the bottom of the stairs he turned, noticed her in the window, and tipped his hat to her. She backed away from the casement, her cheeks scarlet.

Knees shaking, she made her way back to the claw-footed chair and collapsed into it. She rubbed her temples. Good God, she had just done the unbelievable—made another very reckless bargain with the Marquess of Bainbridge. Last time, she had bargained her body. This time the stakes were much higher; this time she stood to lose her heart.

Could she trust him?

Dare she?

Bainbridge ordered his coachman to take the carriage back to the mews at the White Hart; he would walk back to the inn. The stroll would give him the opportunity to stretch his legs and think. Especially to think.

He knew how to charm women. How to sweep them off their feet and make them fall hopelessly in love with him. How to seduce them.

But to make them trust him?

A burgeoning ache throbbed at the base of his skull. How on earth was he going to do this? He supposed he could try to court Kit and maintain a chaste, respectable relationship with her, but that alone wasn't going to secure her trust. She loved him; she had admitted as much, and that would—

He stopped abruptly. A rotund squire plowed into him from behind. In a daze, Bainbridge tipped his hat to the blustering fellow, then continued down Milsom Street. The edges of his vision blurred.

She loved him.

Joy sent his heart into his throat.

Realization turned it around and sent it crashing into the pit of his stomach.

Yes, Kit loved him. But, as he had suspected, her reason held sway over her heart. He must win the trust of both if he was to succeed.

The front windows of a circulating library caught his eye, and suddenly he knew exactly where he needed to begin. He lengthened his stride. He must hurry back to the White Hart; he had letters to write.

Chapter Twelve

*T*he next few days were perhaps the strangest of Kit's life. Lord Bainbridge's marked interest in her brought all sorts of company to her door, mostly the local tabbies who could not wait to collect the latest tidbits of gossip. But these ladies got more than they bargained for; as Kit expected, those who managed to make it past their first encounter with Ramesh nearly fainted when they entered the pagan grandeur of her drawing room.

Kit would never forget the look on Lady Peterborough's face when she told the nasty, insulting woman that the tiger skin on the floor had come from the animal that had killed her husband! It was a complete fabrication, of course, and she had felt guilty for telling such a Banbury story, but it had been worth it to watch Lady Peterborough's eyes bulge as she inadvertently inhaled her tea.

The marquess's continued presence also triggered acts of sheer desperation in her throng of admirers. The sly, reptilian Sir Henry Castleton had take to writing very bad poetry; his latest attempt was an ode to her freckles, and she had tried very hard not to laugh when the man recited it aloud. Lord Edward Mitton had swept her aside at an evening concert and proclaimed his undying devotion to

her. As for Viscount Langley . . . She did not know what
to do about the viscount. He was attractive, dashing, and
witty, and constantly vying with Nicholas—with Lord
Bainbridge—for her attention. Whenever the two men
encountered each other, she fancied she was watching
two tomcats growl and spit and hiss at each other. Oh,
two very polite and well-bred cats, to be sure, but the un-
derlying current of hostility made her skin prickle every
time she ventured into their combined presence.

Then, on Thursday morning, she received no callers. A
trifle odd, given the attention she had garnered of late, but
she was glad for the reprieve. Lord Bainbridge had sent
her a note saying that he had gone on an urgent errand,
but that he should return in time for the ball at the Assembly Rooms. As she had no other obligations, and the
morning was fair and sunny, Kit decided to peruse the
shops along Milsom Street and perhaps pick up a new
book at one of the circulating libraries.

When Lady Peterborough snubbed her in the
milliner's shop, she thought nothing of it. After all, the
lady held no love for her—or for her tiger-skin rug. But
when two other ladies of her acquaintance cut her in the
street while their gentlemen escorts ogled her in a bla-
tantly speculative manner, Kit began to realize that something was very, very wrong. She returned home, her
thoughts in turmoil, to find Viscount Langley pacing in
front of her townhouse.

"Lord Langley!" Kit exclaimed as she approached. "I
must say it is a relief to see a friendly face. This has been
the most extraordinary morning—" She broke off when
she noticed the grim lines on the viscount's face.

"May I speak with you, Mrs. Mallory?" he asked, his
voice low and intent.

"Yes, of course. Won't you come in?"

As soon as they entered the drawing room, the viscount turned to her, his eyes clouded. "I take it you have heard," he said.

She frowned. "Heard what?"

"Ah." He pulled a face and shifted his booted feet.

Kit's frown increased. "Heard what, my lord?"

Lord Langley's jaw tightened. "Forgive me, Mrs. Mallory, for being the bearer of such unfortunate tidings, but a rumor of the most disconcerting nature is flying through Bath society."

"Rumor? What rumor?" But even as she asked, the hairs rose on the back of her neck. The absent callers, ladies giving her the cut direct on the street, the leering stares of the gentlemen. "What is this about?"

The viscount spread his hands. "Please do not shoot the messenger."

"Tell me, my lord, before I lose all patience!"

"Word is being bruited about that you are Lord Bainbridge's current mistress."

She gaped at him. "I beg your pardon?"

A deep flush stained his tanned face. "I did not believe it for a moment, of course, but I thought you should know before you were subjected to any impertinent remarks."

Kit blinked. "Who would say such a despicable thing?"

Lord Langley shrugged. "I do not know how it started, Mrs. Mallory, only that it has spread like the plague."

She lowered herself onto the lion-footed sofa, her eyes wide and unseeing. Her blood ran cold in her veins. Who? . . . Who felt so much malice toward her as to fabricate such a horrible untruth? Aside from their first encounter in the Assembly Rooms, she had comported herself with nothing but the strictest propriety around the marquess. She could not remember anything she may have said or done to give anyone the impression that she had behaved improperly.

"This is unconscionable," she murmured. "I cannot imagine who would do such a terrible thing."

"Forgive my impertinence, Mrs. Mallory," ventured the viscount, "but have you heard from Lord Bainbridge lately? After all, this matter involves him, as well."

"He was called away on urgent business, but he should return this evening. Why do you ask?"

Langley's gaze did not waver. "The marquess has a certain . . . reputation, of which you must be aware."

Kit scowled. "What are you implying, Lord Langley?"

"Only that his 'urgent business' seems to coincide very neatly with the onslaught of this rumor."

"Are you saying that Lord Bainbridge is responsible for this?" she inquired, her eyes narrowing.

"Well, perhaps I am being a trifle hasty in my judgment, but I would not put it past someone like the marquess to manipulate the circumstances to get what he wanted. If he destroyed your reputation, you might have no other recourse but to turn to him for assistance."

"You presume to know him quite well, Lord Langley," Kit noted with a distinct chill in her voice.

"I know only what I have observed, Mrs. Mallory. The marquess usually gets what he wants, by one method or another. How long have you known him?"

"Three weeks. A month, perhaps." Kit shook her head, her pulse drumming an urgent rhythm in her chest. Was Lord Bainbridge behind this? Impossible. He might try to seduce her into marrying him, but these cruel tactics were beyond the pale. He would never do such a thing.

Would he?

He has manipulated you before . . . and lied to you. The last bargain you made with him was a sham. How

*can you be certain that he did not make this second
pledge with you, then take steps to ensure that you had no
choice but to marry him?*

She put a hand to her forehead, squeezing her eyes
shut to try to block out these awful thoughts. How well
did she know the marquess? What was this mysterious errand that had so conveniently taken him away from Bath
at this particular moment?

Could she trust him, after all?

"Mrs. Mallory, you seem unwell," said Lord Langley.
"Would you like me to ring for something? Tea? Your
vinaigrette, perhaps?"

A wan smile ghosted over Kit's lips. "I have never
been the fainting type, my lord. But tea would be most
welcome."

The viscount summoned Ramesh and ordered tea to be
brought to them at once. Then he returned to Kit's side
and perched on the edge of the chair next to her.

"Perhaps it would be better if you did not attend the
ball at the Assembly Rooms this evening," he advised.
Concern shone in his slate blue eyes. "I would not wish
to see you subjected to any impertinent remarks."

Kit grimaced. If the Dowager Duchess of Wexcombe
were here in Bath, she would have nipped such tawdry
tales in the bud. But Her Grace was not here, and Kit
would not disappoint her by showing cowardice.

She raised her chin at a mulish angle. "I refuse to sub-
mit to such a slanderous accusation, Lord Langley," she
declared. "Whoever began this monstrous untruth would
like nothing better than for me to hang my head in shame
and never show my face in public again. I will not give
him—or her—the satisfaction."

The viscount bowed slightly to her, his eyes twinkling.

"I salute your courage, Mrs. Mallory. I would be pleased to storm the breach with you, if you wish it."

"Thank you, my lord. I only hope you do not regret having volunteered."

"I would not call it a Forlorn Hope yet, ma'am," he drawled. " 'Tis only a rumor, after all, and you have many friends in Bath."

"And tonight we shall see just how many," Kit murmured.

Like a medieval knight donning his armor, she dressed with greater care than usual that night, selecting a gown of deep yellow silk that had been made from one of her finest saris; the color seemed to make her freckles less conspicuous. Lakshmi threaded ribbons of gold tissue through her upswept curls. Rather than wear any of her heavy Indian necklaces, Kit chose instead to wear a single teardrop pearl on a filigreed chain.

But nothing could have prepared her for what happened when she arrived at the Assembly Rooms.

As she entered the vestibule with Lord Langley, heads started to turn in her direction. Then the whispers began, discreetly at first, but as they progressed into the ballroom people frowned at her, then murmured to their neighbors as she passed. A few dowagers, like Lady Peterborough and her gossipy set, turned their backs on her. Her cheeks scarlet, Kit allowed the viscount to lead her to her usual corner.

"This is worse than I feared," murmured Lord Langley. "Allow me to seek out reinforcements—Sir Percy, perhaps, and Lieutenant Oddingley-Smythe."

Kit nodded. "Yes, and Lady Arbogast and Mrs. Raebourne, if either of them are here. Both are acquaintances of the Dowager Duchess of Wexcombe, who is a very dear friend of mine."

As the viscount disappeared through the crowd, she

retrieved her fan from her reticule to cool her heated skin. Everywhere she looked, people stared at her, then quickly averted their eyes when she sought to meet their gaze. What was going on? And where was Nicholas? Why was he not here?

"Ah, my dear Mrs. Mallory," said a familiar voice.

Kit stiffened. "Good evening, Sir Henry."

Sir Henry Castleton bowed to her, an oily smile creasing his fleshy face. His dark eyes glittered as they swept over her from head to toe, lingering on her bosom. "A pleasure to see you," he commented, with particular emphasis on the word *pleasure*. "Did Lord Bainbridge not accompany you this evening?"

"No," Kit replied through gritted teeth. "An unexpected errand called him away from town, but I expect him to return presently."

She instantly regretted those words when she saw the baronet's smile widen. "Not so high and mighty now, are you? Just another ladybird in fine feathers." He winked at her. "Do not worry, pet. When Bainbridge tires of you, I will still be here. You will be well worth the wait."

She shuddered as though a slug had just crawled over her skin, then collected herself and favored him with a cold stare. "You forget yourself, sirrah," she replied in clipped tones, then turned on her heel and marched blindly into the crowd.

Lord Langley had been right; she should never have come here tonight. Gripping her fan like the hilt of a dagger, she pressed on through the assembled throng, doing her best to ignore the stares and smirks and sympathetic glances as she searched for the viscount's familiar sun-lightened hair.

Then the crowd seemed to part for her; she darted into

the opening—and met with the venomous blue stare of Lady Elizabeth Peverell.

"Well, Mrs. Mallory," said Lady Elizabeth in a high falsetto tone that carried well over the hum of conversation, "I would never have thought to see you here."

Kit's stomach clenched. "I might say the same for you, Lady Elizabeth." Gracious, what was this spiteful little cat doing in Bath? She thought the girl had been packed off back home.

"Why, I am in town visiting my aunt, Lady Peterborough. I find Bath society to be very improving," Lady Elizabeth explained with a false smile. She surveyed Kit's appearance with open contempt. "With certain exceptions, of course."

Kit's eyes narrowed. "And have you just arrived?"

"Why, yes. Only yesterday."

Yesterday . . . Everything came together. The vicious rumor. Lady Elizabeth's smug smile and the glitter of triumph in her eyes. Lady Peterborough's insidious gossip. Yes, it all became clear as crystal.

"My, you have been busy, haven't you?" Kit murmured.

The girl smirked. "Surely you should realize by now, Mrs. Mallory, that there are no secrets in Bath."

"Even those that begin as outright lies," Kit shot back.

"Lies?" Lady Elizabeth arched a slim dark brow. "You forget, Mrs. Mallory, that I was also a guest at Broadwell Manor. I happen to be very, very observant."

"Observant or vengeful?" Kit snapped. The people directly around them had fallen silent, listening with unseemly anticipation, but that could not be helped.

"I saw you under the tree the day of the picnic," she hissed. "I saw the way you led him on."

She . . . led *Nicholas* on? Visions of strawberries danced

to the forefront of her memory, and Kit felt a familiar wave of heat wash over her cheeks. "You are mistaken."

Lady Elizabeth must have mistaken her flush for guilt; her eyes brightened with fury. "I think not. I did not return directly to the house but stayed near the garden. And I assure you, I could see *everything*."

Kit glared back at her. "If you had seen everything, as you claim, then you would know that nothing happened between us. Nothing except what you fabricated in your jealous imagination."

Lady Elizabeth scowled, then turned to her aunt and said in a very loud voice, "You were absolutely right, Aunt Peterborough. They will admit absolutely anyone to these affairs, even those ladies who are no better than they should be."

Kit stood still for a moment, her shaking hands rolled into fists at her sides. A sharp snap and a brief flash of pain in her palm told her that she'd gripped her sandalwood fan too tightly and broken one of the sticks. Although she longed to announce Lady Elizabeth's role in the dowager's fall to all and sundry, to do so would make her no less a viper than Lady Elizabeth herself. When the dowager duchess returned, she would take the girl down a peg or two. Until then, she must try to hold up her head. What else could she do?

Though she endeavored to maintain her composure, she could only keep her tears in check for so long. The evening was ruined. She struggled toward the vestibule, lost in a sea of censorious, hypocritical faces. A burst of Lady Elizabeth's shrill laughter knifed across her tattered nerves.

A hand touched her elbow, and she jumped.

"Forgive me if I startled you," said Lord Langley. Worry creased his tanned face. "I heard what just happened."

"There are no secrets in Bath, are there?" Kit asked, her voice tinged with a trace of hysteria.

"How may I help?" inquired the viscount.

"Take me home, my lord," Kit replied.

He nodded. "Allow me to get your wrap." He vanished from her side once more, leaving her alone to withstand the assault of prying eyes.

As grateful as she was for Viscount Langley's encouragement, he could not compare to Lord Bainbridge. She scanned the crowd, her arms wrapped around her body, but nowhere did she spy Nicholas's tall, broad-shouldered form. Where was he? Her own shoulders slumped. What was the use? Even if he were here, the whispered scandal would taint him, as well, no matter how vociferously he denied it.

Out of the midst of her upset and unhappiness, a phrase from Congreve hit her like a thunderbolt: *Heaven hath no rage like love turned to hatred, nor Hell a fury like a woman scorned.* Small wonder Lady Elizabeth felt driven by such passion; she had fallen desperately in love with Lord Bainbridge, who had not returned her affection, or even noticed it. For revenge, she had felt obliged to strike out at those she perceived had done her injury. Kit grimaced. "Hell hath no fury," indeed. Now both of them would suffer for her humiliation. It was not fair.

"Here." Lord Langley's gloved fingertips brushed across her neck as he settled her wrap over her shoulders.

Kit started. "Thank you, my lord." Her hands shook. She fought to still them.

"I have sent for the carriage, but it may take some time to reach the front door. Perhaps you would care to wait out in the fresh air," he suggested.

The atmosphere in the octagonal vestibule verged on claustrophobic; the air, redolent with an overabundance of perfume, threatened to choke her. Chills racked her body, alternating with uncomfortable waves of embarrassed heat. She nodded and allowed him to escort her outside. When they reached the street, Kit gasped with relief.

"I fear this evening's events too closely resembled a Forlorn Hope, my lord," she said, clutching her shawl closer about her shoulders. "The occupants of the Assembly Rooms repulsed me from the breach. As drubbings go, that was rather thorough."

The viscount pulled a face. "I regret you had to endure such an unpleasant experience. I only recently escaped similar censure in London."

"Yes, but a lady's reputation is a fragile thing." Tears pooled on her lashes. "Once broken, it cannot be repaired."

Lord Langley took her hand and gave it a gentle squeeze. "Mrs. Mallory, I must confess something to you . . . I hold myself partially responsible for what happened here tonight."

Numbness gathered beneath Kit's breastbone. "Responsible? How so?"

"I warned you about Lord Bainbridge, but I should have been more diligent in your defense. I should have protected you."

Kit shook her head and tried to smile. "No, my lord. You should feel no such obligation."

"I disagree."

"Lord Langley—"

"Please hear me out." He enveloped her hand in both of his. "I should have thought of this earlier. I cannot flatter myself by imagining that you hold any affection for me, Mrs. Mallory, but I would be honored to offer you the protection of my name, if you wish it."

Kit's mind reeled. "W-what are you saying?"

"Eh . . . I am making a muddle of this. Mrs. Mallory, I am asking you to be my wife."

She lowered her eyes. "My lord—"

"Sebastian," he interjected with a lopsided smile. "Sebastian Carr, Viscount Langley, who may not be a marquess, but hopes you will accept him as a poor substitute."

Kit opened her mouth, but another voice—deep, male, and angry—replied for her.

"Good evening. I do hope I am not interrupting anything important."

Kit jerked her hand from the viscount's grasp and whirled. "Nicholas!"

Lord Bainbridge balled his hands into fists as he surveyed the scene laid out before him. Langley, the insolent fop, was gazing lovingly at Kit, and if the marquess had overheard correctly, had just made Kit an offer of marriage. And Kit stood, blushing, eyes downcast, looking for all the world like a demure maid about to accept him. His heart gave a savage twist.

"Kit, I believe the gentleman is waiting for your answer, so please do not hesitate on my account." He bit off each word.

Kit pulled her hand again from her admirer's grasp; her cheeks glowed a brighter red. "Nicholas, this is not what you think."

His lips twisted in a sneer. "No? Did I not just hear Viscount Langley make you an offer of marriage? Really, my dear, it would be quite rude of you not to answer."

She swallowed, and Bainbridge could see the rapid flutter of her pulse in the base of her throat. She licked her dry lips, then turned to the viscount. "You do me a very great honor, my lord, but I cannot accept your proposal."

The viscount straightened his shoulders and bowed to her. "I understand, Mrs. Mallory, even though I am disappointed. I hope you will still consider me your very great friend." The man shot a fulminating glare in Bainbridge's direction.

Good God. Never before had the marquess felt such a strong urge to plant his fist in another man's face. He wanted nothing more than to eradicate Langley by any means necessary, to extinguish his presence from the face of the earth.

"Thank you, Lord Langley," Kit replied. A sad smile lifted the corners of her mouth. "If you will excuse me, I must speak with Lord Bainbridge."

"I shall be here if you need me," replied the viscount with an impassioned look.

"You had better go, Langley," Bainbridge heard himself growl. "The streets of Bath can be dangerous after dark."

Lord Langley stiffened, bowed to them both, then turned on his heel and strode down Alfred Street to his waiting carriage.

Kit turned to him with anguished eyes. "Oh, Nicholas, I feared you would not come."

"It did not appear so to me," he replied. A muscle twitched at his temple.

Laughter sounded from the vestibule of the Assembly Rooms, and she flinched. "Would you take me home?"

Without a word, he offered Kit his arm and walked with her to his own coach. He helped her into the carriage, gave her direction to the driver, then levered himself onto the bench opposite her.

She sat in silence, staring out the coach window, her eyes bright with unshed tears. Something had upset her—

his untimely interruption, perhaps? He flexed his fingers until his gloves strained across his knuckles. He had no idea Langley meant so much to her. All this talk of trust, their bargain, meant nothing.

"I . . . I must tell you something, my lord," she wavered. Still she could not look at him. A single tear tracked a silvery trail down her cheek.

He offered her his handkerchief, taking care that he did not touch her. If he touched her, he would be lost. "Is it about Langley? Do you love him?"

Her head snapped around; the softer curls at her temples swayed with the movement. "No!" she exclaimed. Her nostrils flared. "Why would you think that?"

Bainbridge quirked an eyebrow. "The man proposed marriage to you in the middle of the street. What else should I think?"

She lowered her head, but not before he noticed the way her lips trembled. "No. I do not love him."

"What, then?"

A second tear followed the first. "I discovered earlier today that a vicious rumor about the two of us has been circulating through society."

"A rumor? What sort of rumor?" Doubt tinged his voice.

Kit swiped at her tears. "That I am your mistress."

He leaned back against the squabs, his eyes narrowed. "Lucifer's beard. Kit, I had nothing to do with that."

She smiled, but the gesture held no mirth. "I know, my lord. I had my doubts at first, but tonight I discovered that Lady Elizabeth Peverell is behind it all."

"Lady Elizabeth," he echoed, lips curled in disgust. "I thought she was in London."

Kit shook her head. "No, her father sent her to Bath to stay with her aunt. As it happens, her aunt is Lady Peterborough, one of Bath's most renowned gossipmongers."

He winced. "And she was only too happy to besmirch our reputations."

She glared at him. "*Your* reputation may survive this, my lord, but mine will not. I have never had people give me the cut direct, even when I was married to a Cit. Tonight I have been the target of more cruel and unkind remarks than I wish to count, and I know enough about society to realize that this sort of thing does not diminish over time. I am ruined, my lord. Undone. Dished up."

"And Langley was comforting you." He made it a statement, not a question.

"He was one of the few who dared to stand by me!" she protested. "You were not here, Nicholas—what was I supposed to do?"

"You could have dissuaded him."

"He is my friend!"

Bainbridge's mouth tightened. "And might I also presume that this 'friend' was the one who first suggested I might be behind these rumors?"

"Well, yes, but—"

"I'm going to ask you again, Kit, and this time I want the truth. Are you in love with Viscount Langley?"

"Why do you keep asking me this?" she cried. "How many times must I tell you that no, I am not?"

"Until I believe you," he said flatly.

She paled.

"What would you have me think, Kit?" he demanded. He folded his arms across his chest. "The man flatters and pays court to you all week, while I struggle to keep you at arm's length in order to gain your trust. The moment I leave town this rumor pops up, and he very conveniently makes himself available to comfort you."

"I told you. He is a friend; nothing more."

"Stop being so naive. Men—gentlemen, at any rate—

do not form friendships with ladies. The man is a gazetted fortune hunter, Kit. He wants your money."

"But I have no great fortune."

"You have more than he does."

"I do not love him," she insisted.

"Then why did it look like you were about to accept his proposal when I arrived?"

She glared at him, suppressed a sob, and turned away.

God's teeth, he'd made her cry. The marquess shoved a hand through his hair. All he wanted to do was reach out and pull her into his lap, to cradle her against his chest, to hold her and murmur that everything would be all right. But he couldn't. It was as if a cold fist gripped his heart and squeezed it.

She wiped her eyes again, then swallowed hard. "This has been a misunderstanding, Nicholas. Please, let us not quarrel like this."

The carriage came to a halt at Camden Place; the footman opened the door for them.

Trust. His quest to win her trust had sent him out of town at dawn this morning. It had kept him from touching her all week. But trust cut both ways; only now did he realize how much he had taken that for granted.

Kit had made it clear that she needed to trust him. He had every right to ask the same of her. But right now, he wasn't sure he could.

She had not made too great a point of it, but she had admitted that when the scandalous rumor first reached her ears, she had thought him capable of creating it for his own ends. Selfish he had been, yes, but never would he lower himself to do something so utterly ruthless. He preferred his women willing, not blackmailed. The fact that she had even considered such a thing cut him to the quick.

He levered himself through the carriage door, then

without thinking offered his hand to her. She took it and descended gingerly from the coach.

He could feel her warmth through his gloves, smell her exotic sandalwood perfume as it rose from her skin. Her hair gleamed soft gold in the moonlight.

His fingers convulsed over hers.

"Kit." He held on to her hand to prevent her from climbing the townhouse stairs.

She turned, hesitant. "Nicholas?"

God help him, the way she said his name made his heart turn somersaults. If only he didn't have to do this—

"Kit, I am returning to London tonight."

"Tonight?" she echoed. Her eyes widened. "Why?"

He gritted his teeth and forced himself to say it: "Because we are finished here."

All traces of color fled her face. "Finished? What do you mean?"

He sighed. "You gave me a week to prove that you could trust me. I may or may not have been successful; you must make that decision."

"But the week is not over," she said. Her voice quavered.

"After what I witnessed tonight I realized that trust cannot reside with only one person. I have taken my own trust for granted, Kit. Until now, I assumed that you wanted me as much as I did you. Perhaps that is not the case, after all."

"No," she whispered. "Nicholas, don't—"

He placed two fingers over her lips, stopping the flow of anguished words. "You must decide what you want, Kit. What you want and whom to trust. My presence here will only muddy the waters, so I will give you some room to think. But once you decide, there will be no going back.

"Before I leave, though, I must mention two things. The dowager duchess has returned to Bath; that is the first of my gifts to you. I drove to Broadwell Manor this morning and brought her back. Once she is finished with Lady Elizabeth and the other tabbies, you will no longer have to worry about your reputation.

"The second item is this." He reached into his jacket pocket and pulled out two calling cards. "The first is the card of one Mr. Dalrymple, who owns a printing house in London. I wrote to him about your translation of the *Ramayana*, and he is most interested in publishing it when you are finished. In fact, he is willing to pay quite a sizeable sum for it. You may direct any inquiries through my man of affairs; I have given you his name, as well."

Kit held the cards with shaking hands, tears streaming down her bloodless cheeks. Nicholas reached out and gently wiped them away with his thumb.

"I know how much you value your freedom, Kit," he added, "and I would never dream of forcing you into anything. But I must demand the same thing of you as you have of me. Your love and your unwavering trust. Without those, we cannot be together."

She tried to say something, but the words stuck in her throat. She covered her hand with her mouth and just shook her head.

The marquess took a step back and inclined his head to her.

"Good-bye, Kit." Then, determined to leave before he lost his nerve completely, he climbed into the carriage and ordered his driver to head for London.

Chapter Thirteen

"**G**ood morning!" a woman called from the vestibule. "Halloo? Kit? Good heavens, child, will you tell this Hindu mountain of yours to grant me admittance, or must I languish on your doorstep?"

Kit raised her chin from the arm of the sofa and stared toward the drawing room door with weary eyes. "Ramesh, let Her Grace in."

The dowager bustled over the threshold, dressed in an eye-popping combination of yellow-and-green shot silk. The plumes on her turban bobbed with particular energy. "Eh, what is all this, my dear? I thought your butler was about to throw me bodily into the street."

Kit favored the lady with a tired smile. "I do apologize, Your Grace. I instructed Ramesh not to let anyone in, and I fear he took me at my word. But I failed to tell him that you were the exception."

"Well, I suppose I . . ." She halted midstride, retrieved her lorgnette, and peered through it. "Gracious, my dear, whatever has happened to you? You look as though you spent the night down a well."

Kit wiped the tears from her face with the crumpled cambric square she held in her hand, then rose shakily to her feet. "I am glad you are here, ma'am. I have desperate need of you."

"By Jove, child, I believe you do." The dowager put away her lorgnette, then turned to Ramesh and ordered tea for them both without so much as batting an eyelash. Then she took Kit's hands in hers and kissed her cheek. "What has happened, Kit? Here, sit down beside me."

Kit allowed the elderly woman to press her down onto the lion-footed sofa. She brushed a stray lock of hair from her eyes and took a deep, shuddering breath. How could she even begin to tell the dowager about this tangled mess? About the hurt and betrayal and confusion and longing and . . . And that she had lost the man she loved? She swallowed hard, then grimaced; her throat was raw from the copious tears she had shed over the past several hours.

"Kit . . . have you slept at all, child?" asked the dowager, peering at her with great concern.

"A little. You are in looks, Your Grace," she replied, a trifle absently.

"Oh, this." The dowager waved one hand in a dismissive gesture. "I thought it would be a lark to dress to match my more colorful contusions. I started off with black and blue, progressed through purple and red, and now I am as you see me. A trifle bilious, perhaps, but I think it suits."

Kit sat up, instantly more alert. "Are you well?"

"Of course, child," huffed the elderly woman. "A few bumps and bruises, nothing more. Had the most monstrous headache for days. That old wigsby of a physician says I have the hardest head of any patient he has ever known. Hmph. My grandson could have told him that."

"I am so glad you are here." The crushing weight on Kit's chest seemed to ease.

The dowager patted her cheek. "Tell me, child."

Kit bit her lip. "Oh, Your Grace, I am all at sixes and sevens. I have made a mull of everything."

The elderly woman regarded her intently for a moment. "I have never seen you so distressed, my dear. Does this have anything to do with my great-nephew?"

"Nicholas." Kit's throat convulsed around the name. "Yes, ma'am. It does."

The dowager's lips settled into grim lines. "What has he done now?"

Fighting against the tears that threatened her composure, Kit told her everything, from her first bargain with the marquess at Broadwell through all that followed, culminating with last night's debacle at the Assembly Rooms.

" 'Pon rep, how extraordinary. You should have known better than to bargain with a rake," declared the elderly woman.

Kit smiled through her tears. "Would you believe I did it for you?"

"Next time, my dear, let me fight my own battles; yours are too costly."

"Indeed, Your Grace."

"So where is that reprobate nephew of mine now?" the dowager demanded. "I vow I shall box his ears for this."

"He has returned to London," Kit replied in a dull voice.

"London?" she exploded. "Without so much as a by-your-leave? Bah! How dare he treat you so shabbily! You must go after him, child, and set him straight."

Kit made a moue. "I do not know if I should."

The dowager blinked. "Whatever do you mean by that?"

"I thought he cared for me, Your Grace, even loved me, but now I not so certain."

"Why, because you have quarreled? Egad, child,

everyone has a tiff now and then." The elderly woman settled her skirts around her like a giant bird ruffling its feathers.

Kit shook her head. "No, it's not that. If you could have seen the anger on his face, the disgust . . ." She squeezed her eyes shut as another tear slipped out from beneath her lashes. "He is right. We both are. We may love each other, but without trust we have nothing. And the misunderstanding last night only made things worse between us."

"What do you think made him so angry?" the dowager inquired softly.

"I—I . . . Well . . . I am not sure," Kit stammered. She flung up her hands in exasperation. "No, that is not true."

Ramesh arrived with the tea tray; the dowager waved him away and poured tea for them both. She handed a cup to Kit.

Kit's hands trembled. The cup rattled on its saucer. Alarmed, she set down her tea before she dropped it entirely.

"Take your time, my dear," advised the dowager.

Kit nodded. "At first I thought it was jealousy, because he rang the most dreadful peal over my head for allowing Lord Langley to propose to me in the middle of the street. And I suppose I deserved that. But it goes deeper than jealousy; I know that now. I hurt him, Your Grace. I was wrong to have suspected that he started that awful rumor. I knew, truly knew, that he was never involved, but I think part of me wanted him to be."

"Why?" The dowager duchess was nothing if not blunt.

"Because . . ." Kit worried her lower lip between her teeth. "Because it was safer."

"Safer? Come now, child—you're talking nonsense."

Kit flushed to the tips of her ears. "What I mean is . . . If I had some excuse to break it off with him, I would never risk being hurt again."

The dowager smiled, and a suspicious glint of moisture shone in her dark eyes. "My darling girl, that is what love is all about. If you risk nothing, you gain nothing. But if you risk your heart, you have everything to gain in return."

A fresh wave of tears spilled down Kit's cheeks. "Or everything to lose."

The dowager pried the kerchief from Kit's fingers and presented it to her anew. "This will do you no good clutched in your hand like a rag." She lifted one corner and examined the embroidered "B" sewn there. "Do you believe he still loves you?"

"I . . . I don't know."

"He gave you this."

Kit shrugged. "That is of no consequence. I am certain he has dozens of them."

"What gammon!" exclaimed the dowager. Then, more gently, she added, "Do you love him, Kit?"

"Yes, Your Grace," she whispered. "More than I ever thought possible."

"And would being with him make you happy?"

"Well . . . yes."

"Then why are you sitting here and moping?"

Kit blinked more tears away. "He does not want me."

The elderly woman sighed. "Oh, enough of this missish dibble dabble. Do you love him, or do you not?"

"I do."

"And are you willing to fight for that love? Or are you just going to fritter it away so you can hie yourself off to a convent?"

Kit straightened. "No! I mean, yes. That is—"

The dowager set down her cup with a clatter, then rose

and assumed a businesslike air. "Good! That is something, at least. Come now, my dear, we must move quickly."

"Your Grace?"

The elderly woman looked down at Kit, one cosmetically darkened brow raised in an arrogant arch. "God has given you a chance at happiness, child, and He has put me here to see that you do not bungle it. Now, here. Dry your eyes, and go upstairs and change into traveling clothes. I shall help your maid pack your things."

"Where are we going, Your Grace?"

The dowager rolled her eyes. "Oh, how love can addle the wits of even the most rational female," she muttered. "We are going to London, my dear. And we have no time to waste."

Lord Bainbridge stalked to the sideboard, sloshed the last of the very excellent, very smuggled French brandy from the decanter into his glass, and bellowed for his butler to bring him another bottle. Then, with a snort of disgust, he folded himself once more into the plush wing chair by the hearth and propped one booted foot atop the nearby table. He swirled the liquid around in the glass, watching the play of the candlelight in its amber depths.

He *would* forget her. He must. Or he would run mad. Run mad, and bankrupt himself on smuggled French brandy in the process. Three, five, ten bottles—what did it matter? He sighed and slouched farther into the chair's thick padding.

How had it come to this? He had finally found a woman he loved—loved and wanted to marry, no less—and he had walked away from her. Walked away and not looked back. Had he made the right decision? Or should he have brushed aside her protests and used all the seductive skills at his command to overpower the last of her resistance?

No. He knew that was not the answer; she would never have forgiven him if he had done that. Bloody hell, she had barely forgiven him for the first fateful bargain.

Now Kit was in Bath, and he in London. Was she as miserable as he was? He grimaced and downed a mouthful of the fiery liquor. No doubt Lord Langley had shown up to comfort her. Would that rogue try to kiss her? Whisper in her ear that she was well rid of the reprobate marquess? Would he propose to her again? A red haze misted his vision at the thought. He banged one fist against the arm of the chair. God's teeth, he wasn't supposed to care about what happened to her!

He leaned forward and set aside his glass, then shoved both hands through his already rumpled hair. Lud, he was a mess. No waistcoat, no cravat, his shirt open at the throat. He fingered his stubbled chin. Ah, and unshaven, to boot. How his acquaintances at White's would laugh— the infamous Marquess of Bainbridge, rake and Corinthian *sans pareil*, brought low by a woman.

By love.

He vaulted out of the chair. Damnation! How much more of this was he supposed to take? He began to pace the length of the Turkey carpet. And where the hell was Fulton with his brandy?

Then he heard the butler's voice from the hallway. He cocked his head. His butler's *raised* voice. He frowned. Fulton was as stuffily proper as anyone could ask, and he never raised his voice.

Until now.

"But you cannot simply barge in there, Your Grace!" Fulton protested.

"If you do not get out of my way, you fribble, I shall

not hesitate to take that bottle from your hands and smack you over the head with it. Go on, child. I can handle this upstart."

A lopsided grin slid over his face. Aunt Jo was in fine form this evening. But what was she doing here? His brow furrowed.

The study door creaked open. A familiar golden head appeared in the breach, followed by a heart-stopping pair of green eyes.

His grin faded. Was he dreaming?

"Kit?" The name came out as more of a croak.

"Nicholas?" The vision edged into the room until she stood in the middle of the carpet, her fingers laced tightly in front of her, her eyes huge. A bonnet dangled down her back. Tawny gold curls tumbled about her face.

A dream. That must be it. He must be dreaming. There could be no other explanation. "Are you real?"

The vision smiled. "Yes." She came toward him, and he caught the dizzying scent of her exotic perfume.

No vision, this. His pulse began to hammer in his chest.

"You came," he breathed. He extended a hand to her.

She gazed at him through lowered lashes. "I had to."

"Why?"

She hesitated, then reached out and took his hand. "Because I love you, Nicholas."

With a groan he pulled her to him and buried his face in her hair. God, she smelled so good. He enveloped her in a tight embrace. "I did not think you would come."

Her fingers flexed against his chest; he heard her indrawn hiss of breath. "I did not think you wanted me to."

"Want you?" Bainbridge pulled back a bit and stared down at her, incredulous, his throat raw with unspoken emotion. "Kit, how could I have ever given you the impression that I did not want you?"

She ducked her head. "In the carriage, coming home from the Assembly Rooms. It seems like a lifetime ago."

He nuzzled the curls at her temple. "Ah, Kit." His heart slid up into the back of his throat and stuck there. "I never said I didn't want you."

She gazed up at him through a haze of unshed tears. "I am so sorry. I have made such a muddle of this."

"Shhhh." He moved his lips across her forehead. "You don't need to explain. You are here, and that is all that matters."

Kit pulled back and shook her head. "But it does. It does matter. You taught me that."

He responded with a raised eyebrow.

She flushed; her freckles stood out like dusted cinnamon against her skin. "Weeks ago you asked me what I wanted. Now I know."

He brushed his thumb over the quivering softness of her lower lip. "Tell me."

He felt her shiver, felt his body spring to life in response.

She hesitated a moment, then leaned up and pressed a tiny kiss to the corner of his mouth. "I want you, Nicholas. I want to share picnics in the shade with you, and stories. And strawberries." A teasing smile pulled at her lips. "Lots of strawberries."

The marquess chuckled. "Minx. You forget that I am a rake."

Amusement glinted in her eyes. "A very dangerous and irrepressible rake, so I have been told," she replied.

"Then perhaps it is time I proved to you just how dangerous I am." Tightening his arms around her, he leaned down and claimed her mouth with his.

She pressed herself against him; his blood sang through his veins as her every curve melded with the planes of his body. His mind grew hazy, and all he could think about was how close she was to him and how her skin felt beneath her fingertips, beneath his lips. One hand traced the arc of her spine and came to rest on the upper swell of her hip. A moan escaped her.

He gazed down at her with heavy-lidded eyes. "I warn you, madam, I do not want you as a mistress. You must consent to be my wife. That is the bargain."

She smiled and brushed a heavy lock of hair away from his forehead. "And what do I get in return?"

He leaned down and traced his lips along the line of her jaw. "A lifetime of being cherished and adored. Children. Waking from sleep with the memory of my hands on your body . . ."

She sighed and pulled away as far as his arms would allow. "Behave yourself, sir, or I shall not consent to your terms."

He chuckled. "Yes, you will."

"You know me too well."

"Not nearly well enough. But I look forward to the exploration. Marry me, Kit."

An insouciant smile danced over her lips. "My answer is yes, my lord. Yes, I will marry you."

"Excellent. Now, where were we?" His hand slid down to cup the rounded swell of her breast.

Her mouth rounded in shock. "Nicholas, what are you doing? The dowager is just outside!"

"I know," he replied with a wicked grin. "But she will wait."

Epilogue

*T*he wedding party exited the small church to a chorus of cheers and loud huzzahs as the assembled crowd showered them with grain and flower petals. Everyone in the village had turned out for the event, despite the cool, insistent breeze that ruffled the hems of skirts and threatened to tug hats from heads. No one seemed to mind the inclement weather, for the bride's radiant smile more than made up for the lack of sunshine.

The Dowager Duchess of Wexcombe gave up fretting over the plumes in her turban; they were a lost cause on such a blustery day. She pulled her velvet cloak more closely against her thin frame, guarding against any more incursions by that dratted wind. Hmph. Kit and Nicholas deserved a sunny day for their nuptials, especially after all they had been through. Well, beggars could not be choosers. She sighed. They were married at last, and blissfully happy. That was all that mattered.

Next to her, her grandson, the Duke of Wexcombe, pulled his curly brimmed beaver more firmly onto his brow, then brushed an errant petal from the sleeve of his forest green superfine.

" 'Pon rep, Wexcombe, this is a wedding, not a funeral," the dowager declared with asperity. "You're as grumpy as a tiger with a toothache."

"Forgive me, Grandmama, if I do not share your enthusiasm," the duke replied in arid tones. "I realize you are partial to the chit, but this marriage is hardly cause for celebration."

"You are not happy for your cousin?"

Wexcombe tugged at the cuff of one sleeve. "I would have preferred to see Bainbridge make a more suitable match."

She arched a knowing eyebrow at him. "Like Lady Elizabeth?"

"No, Elizabeth proved far too high strung for—" The duke twitched as though he'd been stung. His eyes widened. "Wait a moment. How did you . . ."

The dowager twitched at the front edge of her cloak. "You need not look so surprised, my boy. I know very well that you and Caroline were scheming to throw that vain, simpering nincompoop at Bainbridge's head. I overheard the two of you plotting together months ago."

Storm clouds gathered on the duke's brow. "Do you mean to tell me that this was your idea?" he asked, clearly outraged. "That you actually *arranged* it?"

The dowager allowed herself a small, satisfied smile. "Oh, pish. You give me far too much credit, Wexcombe; I merely brought the two of them together. Well, I suppose I had to set them straight after your interference, but—"

The duke's lips compressed in a thin line. "And what part did Mrs. Mallory play in this?"

"She knew nothing about it," the dowager replied

serenely. "Although I almost let it slip after that dratted physician dosed me with laudanum. Thankfully, she never pressed me for an explanation."

A stunned expression crossed Wexcombe's narrow face. "Elizabeth. *That* was the reason you took her to task. You wanted to chase her off."

"Well, I could not very well sit by and allow her to ruin things. Another day or so and she would have tricked Bainbridge into compromising her. That *was* your plan, I believe."

He flushed. "You had no right to meddle, Grandmama."

"Poppycock. I was not about to allow you to maneuver Bainbridge into a cold-blooded marriage simply to put an end to his rakehell ways and save you any further embarrassment. Lud, Wexcombe, any more of this highhanded behavior and you will need to have your ducal coronet stretched to fit over your enlarged head."

The duke pinched the bridge of his nose. "But why Mrs. Mallory? Could you not have set your sights on someone more suitable?"

"Suitable?" guffawed the dowager. "I always thought you were pig-headed, Wexcombe, but I never thought you were blind. Why, I knew from the moment I met Kit that that she and Nicholas were perfect for each other."

"I fail to see—"

"Exactly." She waved an impatient hand. "I wanted to see Bainbridge settled, but with a woman he *loved*. Look at them, Wexcombe. Do you not agree that they were meant for each other?"

The two of them turned to watch the bride and groom climb into the carriage; the couple had eyes only for each other. Bainbridge raised Kit's hand to his lips, then turned it over and pressed a kiss to the exposed skin of her wrist. The young lady flushed with pleasure.

"Now," prodded the dowager, "you must at least admit that you were mistaken in your initial impression of Kit's character."

The duke rolled his eyes. "Oh, very well."

"And that you were wrong to treat her with such contempt."

His mouth tightened. "I did what I thought necessary."

The dowager bristled. "Telling Bainbridge that cock-and-bull story of Kit being after my money, then turning around and telling tales out of school to the poor girl—the very idea. You should be ashamed of yourself."

"The chit came from a questionable background, and Bainbridge seemed unreasonably fascinated. I had every right to be alarmed. For that matter, I still have reason to believe he made the wrong choice."

"Oh, stop being such a pompous ass, boy. Bainbridge deserves a measure of contentment, and Kit makes him happy. She is a lovely girl. Pluck to the backbone. She will keep him on his toes."

The carriage began to rumble away, accompanied by the cheers of the assembled villagers. The dowager stood in the churchyard and waved until the equipage disappeared from view.

"Now that this is over," sighed the duke, "I trust you will retire gracefully."

"I have been thinking about that," the dowager replied, tapping a gloved finger against her cheek. "I rather like the role of matchmaker. Perhaps I should turn my attention to your youngest brother, Nigel, or even Lady Elizabeth, although I might be hard pressed to find someone willing to marry a shrew. And since I will be at the dower house for a good portion of the year, I will have ample opportunity to arrange fine matches for Emma and Nathaniel when they come of age. This sounds rather promising, would you not agree?"

"Good God!" blustered the duke, horrified.

The dowager chuckled. Sometimes everything *did* turn out for the best.

Signet Regency Romances from

ELISABETH FAIRCHILD

"An outstanding talent." —*Romantic Times*

CAPTAIN CUPID CALLS THE SHOTS
0-451-20198-1

Captain Alexander Shelbourne was known as Cupid to his friends for his uncanny marksmanship in battle. But upon meeting Miss Penny Foster, he soon knew how it felt to be struck by his namesake's arrow....

SUGARPLUM SURPRISES
0-451-20421-2

Lovely Jane Nichol—who spends her days disguised as a middle-aged seamstress—has crossed paths with a duke who shelters a secret as great as her own. But as Christmas approaches—and vicious rumors surface—they begin to wonder if they can have their cake and eat it, too...

To order call: 1-800-788-6262